THE FIX UP

KENDALL RYAN

The Fix Up

Copyright © 2016 Kendall Ryan

Copy Editing by

Pam Berehulke

Cover design by

Hang Le

Paperback Edition

About the Book

From New York Times bestseller Kendall Ryan comes a sexy new standalone novel.

My tempting and very alpha friend Sterling Quinn is someone I consider off-limits.

It's not *just* that we're friends, he's also cocky, confident, and British, which means he's a walking aphrodisiac.

But lately he's been giving me the look. You know the one. When he thinks I'm not paying attention, and his gaze lingers for too long.

When we start working together, that's when the sexual tension between us gets so thick, I want to hack through it with a machete. I want to make all these deep feelings I've harbored for him disappear, because there's no way this can end well.

The lines between business and pleasure become irrevocably blurred, and I'm stuck between a rock and Sterling's very, very hard place.

Rather than keep a level head about our growing

attraction, Sterling wants to go all-in, showing me just how explosive we can be together.

But I've been around long enough to know that this British bad boy is more than my heart can handle. I'm not about to be cast aside like yesterday's underwear when he's done having fun.

Sterling's never been told no, and he's not about to put his ego aside and play by my rules. But I never thought he'd fight so dirty.

Prologue

From The New York Post:

One of New York City's most eligible bachelors, twenty-eight-year-old Sterling Quinn, is set to receive a long-forgotten inheritance from a distant relative in England, if and only if he marries. The British playboy has six months to wed, and is apparently being flooded with marriage proposals from interested women around the globe.

It's a stunning twist of irony for one of New York's top divorce attorneys, a self-proclaimed confirmed bachelor, and the entire city is eager to see how this will play out.

Chapter One

Sterling

A warm hand grips my cock, stroking unevenly.

I usually appreciate this form of wake-up call, but her choppy strokes leave a lot to be desired. She twists her palm, creating an unpleasant friction. *Seriously, who taught this girl how to toss off a cock?*

"Ow! Fuck." I sit up suddenly, yanking my cock out of her grasp. The damn thing is stinging like he got a rug burn. Her sloppy technique almost makes me want to teach her how to properly handle a man's most important appendage. *Almost.*

"What's wrong, sexy?" she purrs, and reaches for my jutting dick again. The fucker is still hard.

I shudder. *No.* I consider again demonstrating for her. *Curl your palm lightly around, just below the crown, slide up . . .*

"I have an important meeting this morning."

"On a Sunday?" she says with a pout.

Rising to my feet, I grab a pair of sweats from my dresser and tug them on. "I have to be at church in an hour." *I'm totally going to hell for that lie.*

She nods. Her blond hair is matted on one side, not that I can fault her for that; I'm pretty sure I got cum in it last night. Things got a little wild, and apparently I broke my own rule about letting a hookup stay over. Still, I always treat women with respect, so even if she was just yanking on my cock like it was a garden hose, I'm not going to yell or throw her out.

Trust me, she'll be leaving in five minutes, tops, but she'll do so with a pleasant smile on her face, and a *thank you for last night* on her lips.

Why, you ask?

Because I'm Sterling Fucking Quinn, successful attorney, one of New York City's most sought-after bachelors, and in addition to a rather nice appendage, knickers melt when I open my mouth. I grew up in England, and my British accent is like lube. It makes girls wet instantly.

While she dresses, I grab my phone and see I have

forty-two missed calls and dozens of voice mails and texts. Most of them are from my uncle Charles, who I haven't spoken with since the last ten-year family union. And several are from my best friend, Noah.

What in the hell?

I dial my uncle Charles and wait while it rings.

"Sterling, thank God I've reached you. I have some rather shocking news."

My first thought is that something happened to my mum. I pad barefoot out to the living room to give my guest some privacy in the loo. I stand there, phone pressed to my ear, my jaw hanging open and one hand down the front of my pants, checking my sore cock for injuries as I try to comprehend what Charles is saying.

Something about my mother's grandfather, who I never met and honestly didn't know was still living, and a will and millions of dollars at stake.

"Get to the bloody point, Charles. What are you saying?"

"Are you near a TV?" he asks.

I grab the remote and turn the TV on.

An image of my face is on CNN. The picture is one of me smiling in a Yankees T-shirt, taken this summer. It's from my personal social media account.

What the fuck? The newscaster is saying something about an inheritance.

"In a plot suited for the big screen, this is anything but fiction. Sterling Quinn, a New York lawyer, is reportedly set to gain a multi-million-dollar inheritance upon marrying."

I hear footsteps behind me and click the button on the remote, silencing the TV.

"I'll call you back, Charles." After I go throw up.

"Is that you?" the girl whose name I can't recall asks, her eyes widening at the headlines flashing across the screen.

I make a noise of agreement, suddenly fucking speechless.

"You have to get married?" she asks, her voice softening. Cum-Hair Barbie is looking at me with renewed interest.

"Church. I have to get to church," I mutter again. This time it's not a lie. I need to pray to God this is all a dream.

There's no way I'm ever getting married, not for all the money in the world.

Except . . .

I realize with horror how very fucked I am.

Chapter Two

Sterling

"Pick me!" a platinum-blonde in fuck-me pumps calls from the crowd.

"No, choose me! I give great head." A second girl winks. She's got a nice set of cantaloupes too, but that's beside the point.

Reaching down, I pinch the inside of my arm to make sure I'm not dreaming.

Ouch. Definitely not dreaming.

I quicken my pace toward the doors, intent on getting to safety from the mob that's been following me constantly. From my office to the doors of my apartment building, they've been relentless ever since the news broke five days ago. My love life has been fodder for the gossip rags and page-six columns all week, and I'm cursing Uncle Charles for taking this long to get here as I duck my head and ignore the attention.

After shouldering my way through the crowd, I

step inside to the cool air-conditioning and straighten my tie. I've never seen so many hopeful-looking women all in one spot before. Evening gowns, push-up bras, and eyelash extensions seem a bit much for seven in the morning, but what do I know? I feel a bit like the guy on *The Bachelor*. But there are no roses to give out, and this is my life, not some goddamn reality-TV program.

Only once the doors to the lift close do I take a deep breath for the first time this morning. This is insane. *Insane.*

I check the text message on my phone to double-check the location of the conference room, and punch the button for the twenty-second floor.

Did I mention this was insane?

When the doors open, I stroll down the hall, desperately trying to keep a calm, neutral expression. I can't let anyone know I'm rattled by this. Maybe after my appointment this morning, I can swing by and see Rebecca, take the edge off. Nobody knows how to take the edge off quite like Rebecca. She does this thing with her legs; she's a fucking pretzel.

Shit. I need to clean up my image. Quickies in the men's room of my office aren't going to work anymore. I need to start thinking like . . .

My jaw ticks at the thought, and I suppress a shudder. *Fuck.*

A *husband.*

One little word shouldn't make me break out in hives, but as one of New York's best divorce attorneys, the idea of marrying scares the ever-loving fuck out of me.

Regardless, Rebecca is a habit I need to kick. She was someone who filled the void, but it's unfair to let her live on the fumes of hope that she and I can be more. If the scene outside is any indication, I need to get my life sorted out, and that doesn't include banging my ex when I have an itch that needs scratching.

When I pull open the door to the conference room, I spot a familiar and unexpected face. The hot as hell, and just as unobtainable, Camryn Palmer. Her tousled honey-blond waves rest just past her shoulders, and her glossy pink lips form a polite smile. When my family's estate manager, my uncle Charles, said he was hiring a public relations expert, I never would have guessed it would be the gorgeous Camryn.

Just because I've made the decision to do this doesn't mean I have to be happy about it. And the last thing I want is the one woman I can never have in my bed overseeing the whole thing. She's driven and intelligent, but most of all, she's beautiful, which is an added distraction I don't need, one that could be disastrous in an already dicey situation. She also sees right past my bullshit.

"What's she doing here?" I ask as I slip into the chair next to my uncle Charles.

Camryn's wide-eyed optimism falls, and she pulls her lower lip between her teeth.

Shit. Now I feel like an arsehole. Her puzzled expression conveys her confusion and hurt.

Memories of the last time I saw her invade my head. It was at my best friend Noah's wedding. She was the maid of honor; I was the best man. Everything about that night is still crystal clear. The light floral scent of her skin when we swayed on the dance floor during the customary wedding-party dance, her flirty smile and cheerful peal of feminine laughter when I said something undeniably British that amused her.

She was nearly irresistible that night in her long plum-colored gown, her hair trussed up in an elegant twist with fragrant curls framing her face. We shared a dance, some laughs, a glass of champagne. I was thirty seconds away from begging her to go home with me when I saw it.

The way she turned, eager to watch Noah and Olivia share their first wedding dance . . . the unshed tears gathering in her eyes as she looked on.

The excitement and blind faith in her expression was undeniable. She's a true believer in happily-ever-afters, a slave to the idea of lasting love and forevers. I'm a jaded divorce attorney who can tell you every statistic on marriage and divorce over the past thirty years. I can also personally tell you about the lasting pain that endures for years after the split.

And even as jaded as I am, it was a beautiful moment. So I left her alone and let her enjoy it.

I knew a bit of her history. She'd recently come off a bad breakup, and since I refused to further destroy her belief in men, it was final in my mind. She was lovely, but she wasn't meant to be mine.

Camryn will never settle for a one-night stand with a guy who has zero interest in commitment. She's the type of girl who will want it all, and since I'm not the man to give it to her, I wouldn't allow myself the pleasure of taking her home that night. As far as I was concerned, the petite, curvy, and enchanting Camryn was considered off-limits.

Except here she is, blinking at me, looking hurt.

Chapter Three

Camryn

"What's she doing here?" are the first words out of Sterling's full, pouty mouth as he slides into a rolling leather chair across from me.

I can't help but flinch a little at his words.

Sterling and I have always gotten along well, even if he is a pompous player who's too sexy for his own good. There was a time when I hoped he'd ask me out, when I thought maybe he was looking for more. We danced and laughed at our friends' wedding, but that was months ago now.

"She's the one who's going to save your ass," one of his advisors says.

"Morning, sunshine." I grin at him. Fighting the urge to look away from those sexy dark-blue eyes, I hold his gaze, not wanting to let him know how very much his presence rattles me. I cross my legs and straighten the leather portfolio on the sleek mahogany table instead.

Yesterday afternoon, my boss and my best friend, Olivia Cane, CEO of Tate & Cane Enterprises, called me into her office. She'd been contacted by a wealth manager in London about doing some publicity work. I had no idea what it entailed, only that it involved our friend Sterling. I had a feeling the handsome Brit was going to be a major pain in my ass. He was known to be a huge playboy, which I have little time or respect for. But he's stupid hot. As in, he makes smart girls act stupid, so I need to keep my defenses up, and most of all, my legs closed.

"So, what's this big project you said I'd be working on?" I'm more than a little curious about what I'm supposed to help Charles and Sterling with.

The wealth manager, Charles, who also happens to be Sterling's uncle, flew in from London yesterday. And he has one expression on his features. Sheer panic. Sterling stretches and covers a yawn behind his hand.

"As you may be aware, Sterling Quinn is the heir to the Quinn fortune. His great-grandfather Duncan Quinn built a sizeable wealth over the course of his life."

My gaze cuts to Sterling. Heir to a fortune?

Gulping down a huge breath, I try to compose myself. I only know Sterling as a huge manwhore, a sexy Brit, and a cocky lawyer who doesn't believe in love.

"I had no idea," I say, breathless.

Sterling winks at me. "Neither did I, until Sunday morning."

"His great-grandfather recently passed away, and according to his will, everything is to be left to Sterling upon the completion of a few strict requirements. Actually, just one . . ."

Glancing up, I catch Sterling watching me. I wonder if he remembers that night as fondly as I do. Distracted, I clear my throat and motion for Charles to continue.

"To receive his inheritance, he has to be wed. And we have six months to make that happen."

I study Sterling's expression, trying to make sense of his feelings on this. His smirk is amused, as if to say,

Isn't this a fine little mess we've found ourselves in?

I cross my legs beneath the table. He's an attorney, so he makes good money; maybe he doesn't need it. "How many millions are we talking here?"

Charles purses his lips. "Fifty million dollars."

Okay, scratch that. Who's going to say no to that kind of money? *Damn.* No pressure or anything.

My heart starts to gallop. "And you want me to . . ."

I leave the rest unfinished. Seriously, what is my role in this crazy scenario? An impending panic attack lurks under my cool facade. If they think I'm going to be the one to marry him, they've fucking lost it.

"I take it you saw the media circus and hordes of women out there?" Charles asks. "Everyone's vying for a piece of the new millionaire bachelor."

As I nod, my gaze drifts over to Sterling once again. I wonder how he feels about all this, about all the attention. Does he feel like a piece of meat? I would. Those women are nothing but gold diggers looking to cash in. Then again, as a manwhore, maybe he's loving it. Maybe he actually collects thongs as trophies.

"Your role will be to manage this entire process from start to finish. To come up with and execute a plan that ends with Sterling married before the six-month deadline."

Huh. So that explains what I'm doing here.

Sterling's cocky smirk pulls into a full-on grin. "I have to be to court in an hour. Camryn will handle this."

Camryn will handle this? Dude. What in the actual fuck? Does he not understand that the *this* we're discussing is his future, his *wife?*

I'm a PR executive at one of New York City's best marketing and publicity firms. I'm not the fucking millionaire matchmaker.

I'm going to kill Olivia.

Chapter Four

Sterling

"So, what are you going to do?" Noah asks, his smirk smug.

The cocksucker is having a moment of déjà vu. It was only a handful of months ago that he told me about the arranged marriage his father's will proposed, and I was the one mocking him and telling him it would never work. Seriously, what are the odds that two friends would each find themselves in a marry-or-else situation? This is the twenty-first century, is it not?

"There's no way I'm letting millions go. I'm going to do what any normal man would do. I'm getting fucking married," I tell him.

Noah chuckles low under his breath. We're seated at a bistro near the courthouse where I've just finished dissolving the marriage of two nasty clients involved in an intense custody battle. It's disturbing that two people who vowed to love each other for all of eternity, who produced three humans together, could turn so viciously on each other. Then again, I know all of this from personal experience too, which makes it sting all the worse.

I take another sip of lukewarm tea, and try to let it go. But bloody hell, with my own marriage looming on the horizon like a death sentence, it's hard to imagine how I can possibly put myself through something similar. I just have to remember the reason I'm doing this, make a plan, focus on it, and not let anything get in the way, even my own desires.

"You'll be fine." Noah takes a sip and nods at me over the rim of his cup. "Look at me and Olivia."

They're happier than two drunk soldiers at a whorehouse. But they're the exception, not the rule. They've known each other since they were kids, and their fathers had a hand in uniting them, both in business, by naming them co-CEOs, and also in love. My situation is totally different. I'm going to be forced to marry a virtual stranger or else lose out on millions, all because my great-grandfather was old-fashioned and thought that a man of my age needs a wife and family.

"How's Olivia getting on?" I ask, needing a topic

change.

A sappy smile graces Noah's lips, and the bastard lets out a dreamy sigh.

It's better to focus on his happy life than my dreadful one.

Chapter Five

Camryn

"And if I refuse?" I place my hands on my hips.

After that disastrous meeting this morning, I've planted myself in Olivia's office, and I'm not budging until I get some answers. It doesn't matter that she's six months pregnant; I'm not leaving this office until I've made my point.

"You're not going to refuse." She rolls her eyes. "First of all, I know you, and you've never once in your life backed down from a challenge. And second, because I'm asking you to do this, Cam. As your friend." She shrugs. "And as your boss."

I shake my head at her. "So I'm going to be babysitting Sterling for the next six months, helping him to what—date? This is ridiculous. I don't think I can do this."

"Did I mention the client has promised a ten-thousand-dollar bonus if you pull this off?" she adds sweetly.

Ten thousand dollars could change everything for me. I haven't opened up and told Olivia about the whole deal because it's kind of awkward when your BFF is a multimillionaire, but when my last boyfriend took off, he left me with a small mountain of debt. I cringe every time my phone rings, not knowing if it will be another call from a credit-card company. And now I've gotten myself two months behind on rent, just trying to pay the minimum on my credit-card bills.

I never imagined I'd be living like this, my stomach in cramps when I think of my financial landscape. Even worse? I don't have any of the shiny things to show for the money spent. My ex disappeared with my heart, and everything else. A ten-thousand-dollar bonus could pay all of it off. I could start actually sleeping at night again instead of worrying how I'll pay off the credit-card debt he left me.

"I'm listening." I slump down into the firm leather chair in front of her desk.

Olivia places her elbows on the desk and leans in closer. "I knew you'd come around."

"But seriously, how am I going to do this? I have no idea what Sterling wants in a wife, and I still have my other clients and projects to manage."

Olivia leans back and places one hand on the firm, round bump of her belly, stroking lightly. God, why does she have to be so adorable? It's hard to stay mad at her.

"True. Well, I suppose you'll have to spend some extra time with Sterling, figure out what he wants. And I'll tell you what—with what the estate people are paying the firm, I think I can even cover the cost of an assistant for you. Would that help you manage?"

My very own assistant? A small smile graces my lips. "I like that idea. But the idea of hunting out candidates and interviewing . . ." I sigh.

"Problem solved. Anna's firm is downsizing. She'd be perfect."

Anna has been a close friend since the fourth grade. She's someone I adore and trust. Plus, she's super hardworking.

"I had no idea."

Olivia nods. "She e-mailed me her résumé this morning. She just got wind of the corporate downsizing."

"Wow. Tough luck." I know Anna loves her job; she's been there for years. "Okay. Let's do this."

I head back to my office, intent on getting some work taken care of, but first I send a quick e-mail to Anna to set up an meeting for after work tonight.

Just as I begin editing the latest media-campaign graphics, a text on my phone snatches my attention, and I grab it to check the caller ID. It's an unknown number, and I'm about to shove it back into my purse without answering. Probably another fucking bill collector. My ex needs his balls chopped off with a rusty butter knife.

Then I remember Sterling and I exchanged numbers after the meeting this morning.

STERLING: *When do we start?*

No pleasantries, no *hello, how are you?* And on top of that, he just assumes I'm going to take the job. Which I am, but still. Before I can think up a witty reply, he sends another text.

STERLING: *I'm free tonight after work.*

Worse than him assuming I'm going to drop everything and work for him, he assumes I have no life and can meet at the drop of a hat. The cocky asshat.

CAMRYN: *I have plans tonight, sorry.*

Without missing a beat, my phone chimes again.

STERLING: *Tomorrow night then.*

I need tonight to get my act together. I know I can

count on Anna to help me create a winning game plan. Then I'll be ready to face Sterling, ready to face this fix-up assignment head-on.

CAMRYN: Fine.

STERLING: Seven at La Brasso.

La Brasso is a nice Italian restaurant that opened recently, and has been in the news because of some fancy chef and their long waiting list to even get a table. I have no idea how or why Sterling thinks we can get in tomorrow—Saturday night, of all nights—but I don't argue.

• • •

The second I open the door, Anna tackle-hugs me.

"Cam! It's so good to see you." When she pulls back and meets my gaze, she frowns. "You look tired, sweetie." She pats my back.

"Thanks?" I chuckle and shake my head. "No, it's

just work. But that's why you're here."

Anna makes herself comfortable, flopping down onto the plush Pottery Barn sofa I saved for and finally bought last year. But now with money being so tight, I feel guilty every time I sink into the blue microfiber fabric.

"I know, and I'm so excited we're going to be working together. You and Olivia are really saving my ass."

I sit down beside her. "You're saving my behind; trust me. This isn't going to be a typical assignment, or easy."

She smiles wide, the little gap between her front teeth endearingly lovable. "Olivia already filled me in. This is gonna be fun!"

There's one thing you need to know about Anna. She is freaking adorable. Five foot one with bouncy honey-colored waves and an infectious, happy attitude. Seriously, she's the best. And I have a feeling that if I survive the next six months, she will be the number-one reason why.

Anna grabs her purse that's slumped at the floor near her feet and pulls out a stack of DVDs.

When I see that they're seasons one through six of the show *The Millionaire Matchmaker*, I let out a shriek of laughter.

"Oh my God. You didn't."

Anna beams. "Oh yes, I did. We're going to learn from the best, baby."

I'm about to break the news that I don't have a DVD player when I suddenly remember that David's stash of crap in the hall closet includes a gaming system that I'm pretty sure plays DVDs.

"One sec." A few minutes later, I scurry back with the contraption. "Courtesy of David the Douche."

"Ugh. Why haven't you burned this stuff? Or better yet, sold it?" Anna groans.

"I have no idea."

I plug the thing into the outlet near my flat-screen TV. This little black box used to be a huge point of contention in our relationship. He spent more time fiddling with this than he did with me, a point I refuse to dwell on right now. Tonight is about fresh starts and new beginnings. I'm going to be working with one of my best friends in the whole world, and if tonight is any indication, it's going to be damn fun.

We share a pizza and a bottle of merlot, and only make it halfway through season one, but I already have a notepad filled with ideas.

"No sex before monogamy. Genius rule." Anna bites off a hunk of pizza crust, nodding along with the mantra from the show's host and our new girl-crush, Patty Stranger.

"Amen, sister." I raise my wineglass in salute. "This lady is a genius."

Even though this lesson isn't for me, I'm picking up a lot of helpful tips too. For instance, did you know that a man wants a woman who is ladylike, polite, and respectful? It sounds old-fashioned, but apparently it's true. I think it was Ludacris who said *a lady in the street and a freak in the bed.* So in addition to jotting down notes for my meeting with Sterling tomorrow, I write a few reminders for myself. *Don't call or chase after him excessively, and remember to say please and thank-you.*

"I think I'm ready for tomorrow." Surveying the notepad, I lean back and sink into the couch.

It's filled with things like:

First-date kiss—acceptable.

No dick pics—ever. Not even when drunk. That should be another rule—no drunk texts.

No sex on the first or second dates. And that includes oral, mister! I'd like to see Sterling try to stick with that one.

"You're going to kill it." Anna nods.

"So, when do you start working with me officially?" I ask, setting the notebook aside.

"I'm all yours on Monday."

I nod. "Cool. I can't wait."

"Me neither."

After I walk her to the door, we share another hug.

"When are you meeting with Sterling?"

My gaze drifts to the wall behind her. "He asked me for dinner tomorrow night. At La Brasso."

Anna frowns. "Hmm."

"What?"

Shaking her head, she adjusts her purse strap higher on her shoulder. "Nothing. That's just a really romantic, intimate restaurant. I mean, I've heard, but I've never been there. Too rich for my blood."

"I'm sure he doesn't realize that."

I have no idea why I said that, why I defended Sterling and downplayed it. The truth is, I have no idea why he asked me to dinner. We can handle all this through e-mail if we really want to.

Anna purses her lips, studying me, and then nods. "You're right. I'm sure it's nothing."

Awareness prickles at the back of my neck. "I'll fill you in on everything. Talk soon."

And then I'm standing there, tipsy and slightly confused, alone in my apartment.

It's almost midnight, but I'm not tired. I grab the last slice of pizza and my laptop, and scurry off for my bed, slipping under the powder-soft duvet with a sigh.

With a mouthful of spicy pepperoni, I open my favorite social network and type in Sterling's name.

His bright, magnetic smile beams back at me. Despite our close friends being married, he and I aren't all that close. We're acquaintances, at best. I've never friended him, and he's never friended me. Which means my access to see his personal profile is limited. There are only a handful of pictures I can see.

Scanning through them, I decide this isn't technically stalking since I've been hired to work on managing his personal affairs. There's a shot of him and Noah, their arms slung over each other's shoulders at a charity golf event last summer. One from Olivia and Noah's wedding.

Damn, Sterling looked fucking sexy in that tux, but I already knew that. I wondered briefly at the wedding when he brought me a glass of champagne, and subtly flirted in that coy way he has, if we'd be the stereotypical maid of honor and best man who hooked up at our friend's wedding. But it wasn't to be. Sterling left early that evening, looking like there was something on his mind.

It's weird how you can know someone for years, but really not know them at all. I have no idea what his favorite candy is, what type of underwear he wears—or if he even wears any, or what type of movies he favors. I don't know his hopes or dreams. But something tells me I'm about to learn all of that, and a whole lot more. I just don't know if that's a good thing or not.

Deciding it's time to get to sleep so I'm fresh for my date tomorrow, I close my laptop and climb from the warm cocoon of my duvet to wash my face and get ready for bed. Toothbrush halfway to my mouth, I pause, my eyes flashing to the vanity mirror.

Tomorrow is not a *date*. There will be no dates with Sterling Quinn. That little pang of regret in my belly will just have to fuck off.

Chapter Six

Sterling

Most nights I opt for a take-away dinner from my favorite local deli, but tonight I'm straying from my usual fare for a very good reason. Stepping out of the shower, I towel off and pull on a pair of jeans and a navy button-down shirt.

Forced to yank one out under the warm spray of water was a necessity since I'll be dining with a beautiful woman I have no chance of bedding tonight. A fucking travesty is what it is.

Most guys only want one thing, but my needs and desires are a little more complex. Yes, I blow off steam from time to time with a one-nighter, but truly, my mum is now the center of my world. She has early-onset dementia, and making sure she gets the best care possible has fallen to me.

My father turned out to be a self-centered prick. He might have promised to stand by her side in sickness and in health, but when her health started declining three years ago, he took off for greener pastures, saying he was suffering from a mid-life crisis and needed to find himself. Whatever that meant. He hauled off back to London to live with a woman he'd crushed on while in secondary school, while Mum was left to face her prognosis alone.

More than having to make health decisions and pay for her care, it's had an even greater effect on me. My belief in love is totally fucking shot. My parents' marriage was a long and happy one, and then *poof*, he was gone, like none of it meant anything at all.

I've spoken to him all of three times in three years. I know it's up to me to take care of her without having to rely on one dime from him. While I make a good living, this is also New York City, one of the most expensive cities in the world. For now, Mum's at an assisted-living facility in New Jersey, but ideally, I'd like to be able to move her into a better place, closer to the city. That inheritance means I'll never have to worry about taking care of her ever again.

Releasing a heavy sigh, I slip my feet into boots.

I can't fuck this up. I need to get to the end of this

whole process married, just like I discussed with Noah. It's the only way to make all this work.

Yes, I've fancied Camryn ever since I first met her years ago. She's classy and smart and a little hard-nosed, as any good New York businesswoman is. But I've made my peace that since I never got off my arse and made a move on her, that ship has sailed. It's done. Asking her out to a nice restaurant that's sure to impress means nothing.

Running a bit of product through my hair, I chuckle to myself.

Yeah, fucking right.

Chapter Seven

Camryn

The restaurant is spectacular. Dark and moody with a sensual vibe, it's easily the nicest restaurant I've ever been to. Anna wasn't kidding around last night.

After I check in with the hostess, she instructs me to follow her and sashays off for the far end of the building. Apparently, Sterling is already here.

Cream-colored silk drapes cascade from the vaulted ceiling, giving each polished oak table its own private alcove. Supple leather loveseats that are way too big and cozy to be called dining chairs flank each rectangular table.

After passing by half a dozen tables, finally I spot him. Sterling must have requested a private table, because while they are all semi-private, this table is at the back of the restaurant with nothing on two sides but walls of windows overlooking the twinkling city skyline. Sitting beside our table, chilling in an ice bucket on wrought-iron legs, is a bottle of champagne.

Spotting me, Sterling rises to his feet. He anchors one hand to my waist and leans in to place a quick peck on each cheek.

"You're looking particularly fit this evening," he murmurs, sending a warm rush of tingles skittering along my skin. I was glad I'd chosen my formfitting black shift dress; it was neither too casual nor too dressy.

"Thank you. And you look . . ."

Sterling is dressed in a navy button-down shirt that clings in a distracting way across his muscular chest, shoulders, and biceps, and then tapers down to reveal a trim waist. Dark-washed jeans and laced brown boots complete the casual, yet sexy look.

When he raises his eyebrows at me, I realize he's still waiting for the other half of that sentence. Handsome. Nice. Good. Sexy. Lickable. Worse, fuckable. I mean, holy shit, positively rideable.

"Appropriate," I blurt.

A slight twitch in his jaw is the only reaction I get before he slides into his seat.

As flickers of white candlelight dance in the shadows, it takes me a moment to truly get my bearings. How in the world I'm supposed to wine and dine with this gorgeous man and talk intelligently about getting him married off, I haven't a clue. Talk about an awkward situation.

Tamping down a wave of sudden nerves, I lower myself into the seat across from him and swallow the lump in my throat.

This shouldn't feel like a date, yet everything I've rehearsed with Anna flies out the window the second he sits back in his seat and appraises me with those navy-blue eyes, the hint of a smirk still lingering on his lips. It doesn't help that I've forgotten my notebook. Then again, maybe it was for the best. I don't want to look like a total amateur, reading the notes I prepared the night before.

When I'm around Sterling, I feel unsure and uncomfortable. Off-kilter. Definitely off my game. With his chiseled jaw and perfect, full lips that are designed for long, sensual kisses, and hair just long enough on top to pull, it takes me a moment to pull myself together. He shouldn't affect me this way, but it's obvious he does.

Aiming to regain some of the upper hand, I square my shoulders and lean in. "So, what are your intentions?"

"My intentions?" His mouth twitches with the beginning of a smile.

It's beguiling. *Dammit.*

"Yes." I stiffen. "Are we talking Busty Bimbo Barbie who will stick around only long enough to get a piece of your inheritance, and then you annul the marriage and forget the whole thing ever happened? Or true love happily ever after?"

He chuckles, the sound warm and silky. Sensual, even. "It's improper to talk business before we've even had our first cocktail."

He lifts the chilled bottle of champagne from its resting place and pours us each a glass. The golden bubbles fizz and fade quickly as I lift the elegant flute to my lips.

"To working together. Cheers." He raises his glass toward mine before taking a sip.

I nod, acknowledging his toast. Swallowing a sip of the cool champagne, I appreciate the crisp taste. "This has got to be the most *unique* project I've ever worked on."

"It'll be fun," Sterling says.

The server swings by our table, and after a brief glance at the menu, we order the exact same thing, which seems odd given the vast number of choices. Steak, cooked medium-well, with green salad and a glass of red wine.

Once we're alone again, I ask, "So, are you going to answer my question?"

"About my intentions, wasn't it?"

I take another sip of champagne and give him a slight nod.

Sterling folds his hands on the table in front of him and leans in. I have no idea what he can possibly be thinking as his expression remains impassive, so as not to give anything away. "I want to answer that I don't believe in true love. I want to tell you that it's a crock of shit."

"But you're not going to?"

With a shake of his head, he leans back. "No. Given what I do for a living, and the fact that I see couples and families ripped apart and the pain it causes, the last thing I want to do is make a hypocrisy out of this."

That's not necessarily what I was expecting, but it's admirable to hear him say that he's open to this process. I figured it would be just about the money, and he'd only want the woman around long enough to get his cash in hand. Then he'd be free to continue his no-strings lifestyle.

"So you're going to take it seriously?"

"Yes." His tone is unequivocally confident and leaves no room for doubt.

I don't know his motivations, whether they're for love or money, but if he wants to do this, then I'll be here to help him. I have a big job ahead of me, and suddenly I want to do it well, to help him as best I can, unconventional as it may be. It gives me a small measure of peace that I haven't had over this whole situation, and I'm grateful.

Our meal arrives, and as we eat, I find the small talk flows easily between us.

Between bites of tender steak, Sterling fills me in on the basics. He moved to America when he was fourteen. His father had been relocated for work, and so off they set for the good old US of A. He met Noah in boarding school in Connecticut, and they've been best friends ever since. He's close to his mother, but makes a sour face when I bring up his father, so we move along, avoiding that topic.

I wipe the corners of my mouth with my cloth napkin, careful not to wreck my berry-colored lipstick. "I'd love to hear more about what you're looking for in a wife."

Sterling coughs into his napkin as though the word is a shock. "That's a good question." He sets down his knife and fork and pushes his plate away. "And I'll answer it as long as you agree to play along."

"Meaning?"

"This will be an even exchange. If you want me to open up and share, you're going to have to do the same, love."

"And why would I do that?"

He smiles wryly at me.

"And don't say *because I said so*," I add, pointing my fork in his direction.

"Trust goes both ways," he says in that cheerful accent of his. "If we'll be spending time together, working together, I want to know what makes you tick. I need to know that you're not just in this for the bonus money that was promised."

My cheeks heat because that's exactly why I initially agreed to take on this assignment. But I'm hoping Sterling can't see through me.

"I'm a professional in everything I do. I've taken on your assignment, and you can rest assured, I will not back out."

"I didn't say you would. But as long as we're

discussing it, if you'd like to know what I want in a mate, I think you should have to disclose the same."

I roll my eyes at him.

"Humor me," he says.

"Fine." Crossing my arms over my chest, I lean back in my seat. "I want someone driven, motivated, and hardworking. Someone who's easy to talk to. Reliable. Trustworthy and honest."

I take another sip of wine. It's all true, even if I didn't admit the most important, yet secret quality I hold in my heart.

Flashbacks of David seep into the edges of my brain. I knew from the start he wasn't my Mr. Right, but he was an alluring *Mr. Right Now*. Obsessed with working out, he was muscular and fit beyond belief. My friends teased me that he was a meat-head, and maybe he was. But I didn't care, wasn't concerned that he waited tables and washed dishes for a living. I was caught up in the idea of him, and didn't bother to pay attention to the fact that he wasn't interested in building a life with me, that we weren't actually compatible in real, deep ways.

"Your turn," I say.

"A woman who works hard, knows what she wants, and isn't afraid of a challenge."

Sterling's gaze is deep and penetrating, and I find it hard to dismiss that he's looking at me with deeper meaning than just a cursory glance. It's unnerving. But I shrug it off.

"I'll find her for you." My voice is tiny and unsure, but Sterling hasn't so much as blinked, and I can't escape the feeling that he's thinking, *Maybe I've already found her.*

After a moment of tense silence, Sterling drains his last drop of wine. "How do you propose this will work?"

I dab my mouth one last time with my napkin, then lean forward. I almost forgot this was a business dinner. Taking a deep breath, I try to compose myself.

"Here's what I'm planning. With all the initial interest your story drummed up, I don't think it'd be difficult to find you . . . candidates, for lack of a better word. I think the key will be finding quality woman you'll be interested in long-term."

He nods once, his brows pulled together as though he's hanging on my every word.

I lick my lips and continue. "I'd suggest we hold a recruiting event, sort of like women applying for the job of your wife, where they'll need to pass through an initial interview with me before they get green-lighted to meet you."

He chuckles, low and deep, and the sound goes straight to my nipples, making them harden into points. *What the hell was that?*

"Speed dating meets *The Bachelor*," he says.

I nod. "Exactly. I'll need about a month to pull the event together, and that will still give you five months to actually date the woman and be sure this is the right decision."

"Makes sense," he says.

"And you'll prescreen the applicants before the

event so we can make sure only the most qualified women will be there."

"Brilliant. That works." Sterling folds his hands in front of him on the table, and his long fingers are distracting.

"I'm glad you're okay with it." A warm blush creeps up my chest and neck, and I swallow. "But I do have a few rules you're going to need to abide by."

His interest piqued, Sterling pauses, still watching me.

"Your cock will need to stay neatly tucked into your . . ." I pause, and Sterling lifts one dark eyebrow. "Wait . . . You guys call underwear *pants* and pants *trousers*, right?"

"If by *you guys* you mean the British, then yes. We do." His expression is one of amused reluctance. "It's cute to see you get all flustered talking about my cock."

"Keep it in your pants; that's all I'm saying." I can feel my cheeks heating and need to get off this topic. Shit. *Get off* is probably a bad choice of words. There will be no getting off anytime soon. Unfortunately.

"My cock is a big boy. Pun very much intended."
He winks. "I can handle it."

"That's good to hear, because I mean it. If I find
you a good girl to go out with, I won't have you ruin it
by bringing your big boy out to play with her too soon."

He looks amused. "What's your next rule? You said
you had a few."

"My second rule is that you listen to me. My advice
will all be in the interest of getting you married off, so
it'd be wise to try things my way, even if it seems
unconventional." I'm trying not to sound too bossy, but
Sterling merely chuckles.

"I told you; I want this. I need to get married, so
I'm game to do things your way."

"That's good."

"So, how did you feel when you found out you'd
be working with me on this *unique* project?"

"Honestly?" I raise one eyebrow.

He nods.

"I was . . . pissed off." A little chuckle escapes my lips, and I clamp a hand over them. *Shit. Why did I drink so much?* "I'm so sorry. That was inappropriate."

Sterling raises his hand. "Don't apologize. I asked how you felt, and I wanted the truth."

Exhaling, I straighten my posture. "It's just that I felt my skills and talents would be better suited to something more . . . professional."

He nods once as if he understands. "For what it's worth, I'm glad you're on the project."

I wait, hoping he'll continue.

And then he does.

"You're talented, smart, more than capable. Extremely beautiful, distractingly so." His voice is soft, barely above a murmur.

Wait. What? Is it possible that he's attracted to me like I am to him?

That's not something I ever considered, but he's taken me here, been attentive and kind all night. And now he's looking at me with dark, brooding, fuck-me eyes. Maybe this was his way of testing the waters, seeing if there's mutual attraction and chemistry between us.

The thought is dizzying.

I'll have to tread carefully, make sure I keep this strictly professional. It's not that I'm opposed to a fling, simply because we work together and it may get awkward. No, I'm opposed to a fling because this man will be married in under six months' time, if I do my job well, and I always do. I'm not going to be stupid enough to get involved with him and then end up with a broken heart when he rides off into the sunset with someone years younger, twenty pounds lighter, and of course, millions richer than I'll ever be. No fucking thank you. My ego isn't robust enough to withstand such torture.

Besides, I do have the bonus money to think of. Between the bill collectors calling me and being behind on my rent, I can't overlook the fact that I've landed in a precarious situation, one I'm desperate to get out of.

"What's next?" he asks finally.

"Now that I know what you're looking for, I want

to take some time to create a comprehensive game plan. Why don't you come by my office on Monday, and we can go over everything?"

He pulls his phone from his pocket and checks his schedule. "I'm slammed at work next week. Are you free in the evening?"

"Yes, that might work perfectly. Meet me on Thursday at nine at Ex's and Oh's nightclub."

"Fine. Thursday it is, then."

It will actually give me the chance to see him in his native environment, understand which types of women he's attracted to and watch him in action. And then I can develop a plan that will totally knock his socks off. Which is exactly what I plan to do.

"Shall we go, then?" he asks, and when I nod, he helps me from my chair.

There is just something so elegant about him. Maybe it's because he's British with his accented English and proper grammar, or it could be because he's ridiculously attractive with his stylishly messy hair, square jawline, and tall, muscular physique.

His intelligence is sexy too. I know from poking around online that he's a brilliant attorney who skated through undergrad and law school with impressive ease. Meanwhile, most days I feel like a hot mess. Sniffing the wrinkled clothes piled on top of my dresser to see if they can get one more wear out of them, and crunching on dry cereal on my way to work. I'm guessing that the deliciously well-put-together Sterling Quinn never has that issue.

I need to find him a classy woman. Someone smart and equally as well put together. He's an educated man, and it's refreshing to hear that he wants someone who is his equal. He's not intimidated by intelligence; in fact, he welcomes it. The idea of someone to spar with, to hold a stimulating conversation with, excites him.

This will be my mission: to find him someone great. I just hope, in turn, it will force the not-so-innocent thoughts I harbor for him from my brain.

I shared more than I wanted to divulge tonight. Is it this sexy, sensual man who opened me up like a flower in bloom, or is the wine to blame?

Sterling kisses the back of my hand like a perfect

gentleman, and tucks me inside a waiting taxi.

I watch, wistfully, as his form grows blurry in the distance.

Chapter Eight

Sterling

Thursday night, I head upstairs to the rooftop bar of the nightclub where Camryn suggested we meet. I've arrived early, wanting to get a table so I'm ready when she arrives.

It's not a place I frequent regularly, but I've been here once or twice over the years. Its clientele is mostly single twenty-somethings looking to cut loose after a day at work. A sleek long stainless-steel bar top runs the length of one wall, bar stools lining it. Instead, I choose one of the high-top tables that sit under strands of white lights. The evening sky has turned dark, and the night air is cool but not yet cold.

This week dragged by at a snail's pace. Between work and seeing the inside of a courtroom more times than I would like, I'm tired and on edge. It didn't help that my uncle called almost daily inquiring about updates, and hopeful women still flocked, following me wherever I go.

But then I see Camryn heading up the stairs, and my sour mood drifts away. Strange how she has the ability to do that without saying a single word.

I rise from the high-top table and raise my hand in a wave. She spots me and smiles, a wide grin that reaches her eyes, before catching herself and fixing her mouth into a line again. But I saw it, her raw and honest reaction to me.

"Hi, Sterling," she says while I pull out her chair.

"Hello, love. You look lovely this evening."

Her light floral scent drifts up to tease me while I help her into the seat. Her hair is loose over her shoulders, and she's dressed in jeans and a black top cut low enough to let me catch a glimpse of the swell of tempting cleavage.

The waitress swings by our table, and Camryn orders a fizzy champagne cocktail while I request a gin and tonic.

We make small talk by discussing our work weeks, and Noah and Olivia, and then it grows silent for a minute.

"So I know we know each other, but tell me more about you," she says.

"What do you want to know?"

"Let's see. You're British. You like drinking tea. Before he got hitched, you and Noah wreaked havoc on ovaries around the city."

"True, true, and fuck yeah."

"God, you are crude," she says with a chuckle.

"Hey, you brought it up. But yes, love, I like pussy."

Her cheeks flush, and I give zero fucks about making her blush. There's something in me that likes getting a rise out of her. In fact, I'd love to rile her up even more.

"As riveting as it is to discover you like the hole between a woman's legs—"

"You can say the word, princess," I say with a laugh.

She rolls her eyes. "Pussy. There. Are you happy?"

Grinning at her, I lean back in my seat. "Very."

"So you say you're ready to get married, but have you ever even had a long-term relationship?"

"I have," I say. But that's a story for another time.

Camryn doesn't press me; she just takes another sip of her cocktail.

"Do you want kids someday?" she asks.

I rub the back of my neck. With kids comes a total life change. And until now, my life has been about me. Pursuing my career and the self-interests that bring me pleasure. Though I suppose when I get married, that will have to change too.

"Not sure. You?"

She smiles. "I do, actually. I'd like at least one. A little mini-me, someone to be my best friend."

I can picture Camryn as a mother. She'd be one of those effortlessly cool mums. Not one of those with a gigantic diaper bag, mom jeans, and a permanent look of worry etched into her features. She'd make it fun. I have no doubt about that.

"I don't have any siblings," she continues. "So I guess I like the idea of building my own squad." She giggles, and I wonder if the champagne cocktail she finished has gone to her head.

I signal the waitress, ordering another for her.

"That's something you and I have in common. Only child," I say, motioning to myself.

She meets my eyes, studying me carefully.

The idea of family is something I hold dear, and there's something inside me that warms at hearing her say she wants to build a family. When my own happy family was split apart, I pretty much gave up all interest in the idea, but I'm starting to realize that with the right person by your side, anything is possible.

Camryn's gaze drifts to the dance floor, which on a weeknight isn't being used, but a group of girls in short cocktail dresses linger near the edge. I've paid them no mind, but it's been hard to ignore the fact that they keep looking in our direction.

"They're wondering what a man like you is doing with a girl like me," Camryn says, her voice uncharacteristically soft.

"What do you mean by that?" If she's going to put herself down, I'll have something to say about that.

She shrugs. "It's fine. I'm not bothered by it. You're attractive, and they're interested. Simple as that." She grabs her fresh drink, slowly draining it all, and I get the sense that she's embarrassed.

"Fuck that." I rise to my feet. "Come on."

Chapter Nine

Camryn

I'm out with Sterling at the rooftop bar I suggested we meet at tonight. And though I try to ignore it, I can't pretend the women ogling him don't exist. He's tall, deliciously attractive, and his commanding presence coupled with his British accent make him a magnet for women. That's a fact.

I just didn't expect it to bother me. I'm his matchmaker. He and I aren't here on a date.

"Where are we going?"

"Out of here," is all he says.

He grabs my hand, and as we pass, it's impossible to ignore the group of girls giving me a death stare. His grip on my hand is tight, certain, as though he's not planning to let go anytime soon.

When we stop on the street with cars and taxis zooming past, Sterling still hasn't let go of my hand.

"Don't let those girls bother you." His tone is uncharacteristically soft.

I shake my head. "I'm a big girl, Sterling. I can handle the truth. Honestly, I'm fine."

"You may not realize this, sweetheart, but once upon a time, I wanted to hook up with you."

He takes a step forward and my heart lurches. Unsure what to do with this information, I chew on my lip.

"And you don't anymore." I place my hands on my hips and watch him.

He pushes his hands into his hair, looking eager, yet unsure. "I'd bend you over this rubbish bin right now if you'd let me."

At this, I crack up laughing. Not only does he call a trash can a rubbish bin, which is adorable, but he suggests that we have sex on the sidewalk.

But mostly, I'm smiling because this sexy, confident, delicious man just told me that he finds me attractive. And more than that, he came to my rescue. In my experience, that isn't something that men do anymore.

Last year when a bitchy waitress messed up my order twice and then suggested I was hard to please, David only laughed. I have a feeling that Sterling would have jumped to my defense, maybe even stormed out of the restaurant without tipping just to prove his point. David ate his tuna-salad sandwich while I sulked, waiting for my omelet to be remade. The jerk didn't even offer me any of his fries.

Sterling tosses me a flirty wink, and I realize I still haven't responded to his offer for public sex.

"As fun as that sounds, I think I'll pass." I elbow him in the ribs, and he chuckles.

"Come on."

He takes my hand again and tows me off down the street. We walk for a long time, passing by little bakeries, family-owned restaurants, and dry cleaners while the city buzzes around us. We talk about family, and life, and our goals for the future, and I realize how much I've been missing the thoughtful conversation between a man and a woman.

Chapter Ten

Sterling

I grab my phone and dial Noah, watching as Camryn's taxi carries her into the night.

"So, Camryn's pretty fucking hot," I blurt, my filter gone along with that last cocktail.

But holy shit, she really is. Tonight after leaving the bar behind, we walked and talked, and as simple as that sounds, it's much more than I've shared with a woman lately.

Noah chuckles, and I hear Olivia shout something incoherent in the background.

"Oh my God! Do you like her? Like *really like* her?" Olivia asks excitedly.

"Fuck me. I'm on speakerphone, aren't I?" Rubbing the back of my neck, I wait for Noah to answer.

"Sorry, buddy. Give me a second."

I hear him speak in a hushed tone to Olivia, and then a click as he switches it from speakerphone.

"What in God's name are you talking about?" he asks.

I stroll down the sidewalk, hoping the fresh air will help clear my head. "Would it be the worst thing in the world if I pursued Camryn?"

"What are you saying?"

"Camryn," I repeat. She's hot. She's funny. Feisty. Smart. Why the fuck not?"

"Yes, I see where you're going with this, good buddy, but did you forget about the inheritance? You're supposed to get married."

"Yes, I know that. And Camryn's supposed to help me."

"Sterling, you're going to have to dumb it down for me. I just spent the last three hours looking at paint colors with names like weathered moss and mossy linen. What are you saying? You want to date her while you're looking for your wife? Have you lost it, buddy?"

Rolling my eyes at my friend's idiocy, I hit the button for the street signal. "I'm saying, what if I continue working with her under the guise of finding a wife, but really, I'm wooing her."

Silence.

"Noah?" I pull back the phone and glance at it for a second, wondering if the line went dead.

"I think it's ridiculously stupid," he finally says.

I hail a cab at the corner, and when one stops, I hop inside and direct him uptown. "How so?"

Noah scoffs. "If you like her, just tell her how you feel. Man up; ask her out for real."

"That won't work. First, there's no way Camryn is going to just quit. She wants to see me get that inheritance, and of course, she wants her bonus at the end of this."

Noah scoffs, but he knows I'm right.

There's no way I'm walking away from my inheritance, and for what? A shot at a date? That would be crazy. Not when my mum is counting on me.

And there's absolutely no way Camryn will agree to date me if she knows I'm still planning on getting married at the end . . . but I have no choice in the matter.

It must be the alcohol talking, because I sound crazy. I give Noah an excuse and shove the phone in my pocket. I really need to get my head in the game.

Once back inside my apartment, I leave the lights off, finding my way in the darkness easily. It's an open-air loft and essentially just one big room. Sidestepping around the dining table and sofa, I find the wall that separates my bedroom from the living area and enter my room.

Reaching down, I grip my cock that has been hard ever since Camryn walked up the stairs to the bar, her bottom lip pulled between her teeth. *Fuck.* The soft swell of cleavage under her low-cut top was mesmerizing. And the way she challenged me, probing, trying to tease out what I was looking for. She's inquisitive, open, outspoken. Beautiful. The way she stood up for herself when those women made her feel inferior. I still feel as though I'm in a fog.

I strip my shirt off over my head, and tug my boxers and jeans down my thighs.

My erection stands tall and ready, and I stroke in quick pulls, right there in the center of my bedroom. Needing to relieve tension that her unexpected presence in my life is causing, I move my hand up and down in even strokes, my breath pushing past my lips with the exertion.

With thoughts of Camryn swirling in my brain, my climax comes faster than I expected, and I come in the wadded-up T-shirt still clutched in my hand.

I throw the shirt away because I don't want to deal with that shit come laundry day, and get cleaned up. Sinking into my king-sized mattress, I let out a heavy sigh.

What the fuck is happening to me?

That orgasm didn't even come close to taking the edge off. I'm still keyed up. Yet the text message from Rebecca, that I'm sure is a booty call, holds no appeal. I shove my phone aside without responding.

For years, the only thing I was sure of was that I

never wanted to get married, and now that I'm faced with the fact that I need to, the one girl who suddenly looks very appealing is the only one I can't have.

Of all the fucked-up situations to find myself in, this is one I never imagined.

Noah was right. Asking Camryn out would be insane. It would be suicide. She'd call off this whole thing, and I'd be worse off than I am now. I'm building toward my goal of being able to take better care of my mum. I need to remind myself of that.

Lying there, staring up at the ceiling fan whoosh in lazy circles, I try to solve the puzzle buzzing through my brain. Do I really like her? Or do I only want her because she's the one thing I can't have right now?

Maybe it's only the latter. Maybe she's merely a good distraction for the shit show that is my life at the moment.

Running a hand through my hair, I know that's not it.

At least, I'm fairly certain it's not.

I like her. Deep down, I really like her.

Lying here in the dark cloak of night, I make a deal with myself. I can spend more time with her—hell, I can even mess around with her if things come to that point—but I promise myself one thing. I won't hurt her, won't lead her on and make her believe this could be more. I'm going to be married in the next six months, and I know that true, everlasting love is a false promise that only lovesick fools would believe in.

Life doesn't fucking work that way.

Chapter Eleven

Camryn

It's Friday afternoon, and I'm at the office.

Being the good (nosy) friend she is, Anna has already sufficiently grilled me about my dinner out with Sterling this past weekend, and of course, our evening out last night. I downplayed the strange sexual tension that crackled between us.

The intimacy of the restaurant. The way his gaze stayed glued to mine. His low voice.

My cock is a big boy.

A shudder zips through me at the memory.

And then last night, the way he only had eyes for me, despite the roomful of gorgeous women clamoring for his attention.

There's just something magnetic about him. Of course he's attractive, but it's so much more than that. His confidence. His candor. It's all so intriguing.

If we were both single, I could see myself falling fast for him.

Well, we are both single, but it's more complicated than that. He's trying to get married, and I've sworn off men.

We discussed him swinging by the office today if he got a break in his work day. I'm sure we covered everything last night, but just in case there was anything we forgot, he insisted.

Now that he's almost due to arrive, my heart is in a frenzy, and I swear I've typed and deleted the same sentence three times. Slamming my fingers against the keyboard, I manage to finish the e-mail without typos and finally click SEND.

"You okay?" Anna asks.

Letting out a frustrated sigh, I nod. With the last-minute arrangement to bring on an assistant, I've spent a good part of the week getting Anna up to speed on all of my current projects, which means I've fallen behind big-time on answering e-mails and voice mails. But Anna's a quick study, and is already off and running on creating a mock-up social-media campaign for a client that I'll review tomorrow.

We're sharing an office space, which is fine by me. I have a desk in the center of the room facing the door, and Anna is seated at the L-shaped desk in the corner, typing away.

I refuse to glance up and check the clock yet again, but when I hear a British accent, all bets are off and my gaze flies to the door.

Sterling's in the hall, talking to Noah and Olivia. Today he's dressed in a tailored navy-blue suit with a crisp white shirt and pale pink tie. Only a confident man wears pink.

A warm shiver passes through my body. *Dear God, he's attractive.* He's shaking hands with Noah and laughing about something.

I rise to my feet and wander out to join them. As I approach, Sterling turns to Olivia and gestures to her belly.

"May I?"

She shrugs. "Most people don't even ask. Go ahead."

He places one large palm against her belly and grins at her, his eyes crinkling in the corners. "Wow. This is incredible." Pulling his hand away, he shakes Noah's hand again. "Good job, mate. Makes me want to get someone pregnant."

He chuckles, and I see several of the office girls smile in his direction while my ovaries do a dance of joy.

Get in line, ladies.

I approach and stop beside Olivia. "Hi, guys."

Sterling's gaze pulls over to mine like we're two sides of a magnet. "Cami," he says, his voice low.

"Are you ready to go over the plan?" I ask.

Noah and Olivia are watching us wide-eyed, and while I'm trying to figure out what's up with their weird vibes, Sterling nods and says cheerio to Noah and Olivia before following me into my office.

The space seems smaller with his masculine presence looming.

Anna turns and her focus lands on Sterling, her gaze drifting up his six-foot-plus form. Her mouth opens and she just kind of stares blankly.

"Anna, this is Sterling Quinn. Our new *client*," I say pointedly.

This snaps her from her likely erotic daydream, and she manages to say a shaky hi.

"'Ello, love," Sterling says brightly.

"Go ahead and have a seat." I indicate the floral-print accent chair in front of my desk.

Sterling obeys, and I sit across from him. The desk between us feels like a necessary barrier.

"I made some progress on our plan this morning, contacting a few local hotels to obtain quotes on renting ballroom space for our recruiting event. I think we'll have a good turnout, and we'll need the space."

He nods along.

"I'm aiming to hold the event about four weeks from now. Make sure your calendar is free."

"Of course," he says smoothly.

"As soon as we have a firm date and the location nailed down, I'll begin placing ads on the local dating sites to solicit candidates. After I screen them for the obvious stuff, like making sure they don't have any felonies, or an ex-husband they tried to mutilate, you can have a look at the prospects and let me know if any of them suit you."

He nods again. "Very thorough, Miss Palmer. I'm impressed. You've thought of everything."

"Well, not everything." I realize we never discussed specifics. Last night, we merely covered big-picture things. "I need to know the shape and size of the woman you desire. Age. Hair color. Chest size. Shaved bald or landing strip? Give me your preferences."

"Pardon?" He scoffs with a smirk.

"Be as specific as possible." I grab my notepad and pen, poised and ready.

He leans back in his seat and appraises me, his gaze sinking slowly from my loose chignon bun to the peep-toe pumps resting under my desk.

I fight off a shiver. Good fucking golly, it's been way too long since I've been laid.

"Hmm. Let's see." He leans closer, his eyes still appraising me as he rubs his chin. "Five six." He stops and looks down at my heels again. "No, five three, about 145 pounds. Twenty . . . six? With dark blond hair. Shoulder length. And green eyes."

Sterling just described me to a fucking T, and I'm not amused. He promised to take this seriously.

"Are you trying to be funny?"

"Not at all. Why?" He shifts closer still, and I catch a sniff of his mouth-watering cologne.

"I'm not an idiot, Sterling. You don't need to stroke my ego, or butter me up. I'm in this until the end. When I take on a project, I always see it through. No matter what."

His confused look tells me his compliment had nothing to do with kissing up. Which means now I'm the one who's confused.

Sighing, I inhale deeply. "Okay, let's try this again.

Your preferences."

He rises to his feet and leans over one side of my desk, fiddling with my unicorn mug that serves as a pencil holder. "Size doesn't matter."

"Oh, come on." I roll my eyes and snatch the mug from his hands. "That's just a lie women tell men; you don't need to perpetuate it. Trust me; size matters."

"Fine, does this help? I'd much prefer a Kim Kardashian body type than a Kate Moss."

Okay, so he likes curves. "Yes, it does, actually."

My round, size-eight ass and full breasts usually feel like too much, but with that one statement, my constant *the diet starts Monday* mentality suddenly seems insignificant. I set down the mug on the far end of my desk and jot down a note, then press on.

"Okay. Race, religion, politics . . . anything important I should know? Any particular quirks, such as a foot fetish or a breast man, things like that I need to be aware of?"

"Not really," he says with a chuckle. "I'm fairly

open."

"Well then, I think I have enough to work with for now. I can begin assembling some candidates for you to consider."

Sterling rises from the chair and stalks straight toward me. "One more thing, love." His voice is low, and the sultry sound goes straight to my clit. "Preferably bare," he adds in barely a whisper.

My knees tremble, and I force a breath into my lungs.

"Are you going to write that in your little notebook?"

"I think I can remember that." Actually, I don't think I'll ever be able to forget that detail.

Sterling checks his wristwatch, a platinum-and-gold number that looks expensive. "Are you free Wednesday night, by chance?"

"For?" I thought we were through here.

"To hang out."

Hang out? I doubt that's a good idea. "Oh, I, um. I need to check my schedule."

He rises to his feet, then nods. "Brilliant. Ring me and let me know."

I'm in a daze, but I find myself rising and nodding back at him. "Have a good evening."

"Good-bye, Anna," Sterling says on his way out the door.

I'd totally forgotten about Anna.

"Ho. Ly. Shit!" Anna blurts the second he's gone. "That was freaking intense!"

I want to blow her off, to downplay what just happened. Instead, I lean against the side of my desk and pull deep breaths into my lungs.

"Seriously? That was crazy. I need a cigarette right now," Anna says, smiling at me. "And I don't even smoke."

"Don't read more into this than is there. He's charming and was just trying to be funny. That's all."

I fall back into my chair and try to focus on my laptop screen. But it might as well be written in Mandarin for all I can decipher. Sterling has left me completely and utterly flustered.

"He wants to *hang out?*" Anna giggles. "Is that a euphemism for something sexy where he's from?"

"Of course not; don't be silly." But hell, part of me wants to google it just to be sure. "Let's just get back to work."

Anna sighs, but heads back to her desk.

I can't help but wonder about his past. How many lovers has he had? I don't know his dating history, and when I asked if he's ever had a real relationship, he didn't give me a full answer. I only know about the string of one-night stands he's had over the years. He's never been obvious about it, but I've gathered enough from hanging around Olivia and Noah to understand that Sterling has no problem taking a different woman home every weekend.

As my curiosity grows, I try to convince myself I'm only interested in the details because of my role.

Who am I kidding?

Not Anna. And not myself.

Jealousy bubbles up inside me, and I want to know who he's dated, who he's slept with. Closing my eyes for a second, I scold myself silently, because I have no right to be jealous.

"So, are you going to do it?" Anna asks, interrupting my sour thoughts.

"Do what?"

"Hang out with him?"

Chewing on my lip, I consider it. "I don't know. I might . . ."

"Then you should totally do it." Anna nods.

I can see where her loyalties lie. First, I need some answers.

I grab my cell and dial Sterling's number.

"Hey, Camryn. Did I forget something at your office?" he asks.

"No, I just . . . I had some questions for you."

"Of course. What's on your mind?"

"Well, when you said *hang out*, what did you mean?"

Anna's hand flies over her mouth and her eyes widen.

No sense in beating around the bush.

I can almost hear the smile in Sterling's voice when he replies. "What do you want it to mean?"

Straightening my shoulders, I sit up taller in my chair. "Oh no, you don't, mister. Before I agree to spend time with you, there are a few things I need to know."

"Go for it."

"How many women have you slept with?"

"Pardon?" Sterling coughs.

Anna is on her feet, making slashing motions across her throat with her hand.

"Your number. What is it?" My tone is calm,

controlled. I'm actually enjoying this.

"Is that information you need as my publicist, or as the woman I've asked to hang out?"

"Just answer the question, Sterling. Or can you not count that high?"

He lets out a sigh, so brief I can barely hear it. For a second, I'm sure he's going to dodge the question.

"Enough to know what I'm doing. Not enough to make me a total fucking wanker."

I laugh, despite myself. It's actually a good response.

"Let me make this clear for you. I like you, Camryn. We're both adults, and there's no reason why we can't hang out and enjoy each other's company without it turning weird."

What the hell does that mean? I'm more confused now than before. Maybe this is his last hurrah before becoming a married man.

"I'm not quite sure what to say."

"We have fun together. Let's keep it casual and fun; we both deserve that."

The man has a point.

"But you're about to be married," I say.

"Not tomorrow. Not the next day."

"But soon."

He exhales. "Yes, and that's kind of stressing me the fuck out, so I could use a little downtime with someone who gets me."

I swallow.

"Say yes," he murmurs.

"Sterling . . ."

"I would never hurt you," he adds softly.

"Fine, but I'm not having sex with you."

Anna is now lying on the floor of my office, her face scrunched up in agony, her head in her hands.

"We'll see," he says.

A girly bubble of laughter escapes my lips, and I clamp a hand over my mouth. I want to bitch-slap myself for that outburst. But Sterling only seems amused.

"Seriously, don't worry. Don't overthink this. Everything will be fine," he says. "I promise."

I straighten my shoulders. "Okay then. Wednesday. Where should I meet you?"

Anna breaks out into a huge grin.

"My flat. At seven."

Sterling's sexy deep voice sends a tingle down my spine. My cheeks are bright red when I hang up the phone.

His *flat*. It's cute that he calls his apartment a flat. How very British of him.

Anna lets out a small squeal as she jumps up.

I hold up my hand. "Not one fucking word."

"Poop stick," she says and sticks out her tongue, but goes back to her desk.

I spend the rest of the work day trying to make peace with his explanation, to talk myself into this non-date. I weigh the pros and cons, push the women of his past (and future) out of my mind. But I hate the thought that past girlfriends know intimate details about him—how he tastes, how he fucks, how it feels to sleep beside him all night—all things that I will never know or get the chance to do.

I say good night to Anna and pack up my things. The entire way home, I argue with myself. Part of me wants to just go with it. The other part of me knows this is a recipe for disaster.

My e-mail is full with the first round of applicants, and I know I'll be spending the evening with a big glass of wine and a bunch of women who could be Sterling's future wife.

I'm just going to have to tell Sterling. Our hanging out is stupid. Not when there's so much on the line.

I take a deep breath and remember that he promised it was casual fun, nothing more.

Don't make a big deal out of this.

But it feels impossible not to.

Chapter Twelve

Sterling

At ten to seven on Wednesday night, I take one last glance around my flat. It hasn't been this spotlessly clean since . . . well, ever, probably. I straightened, dusted, vacuumed, and sanitized for the last hour and a half.

My balcony, which was the whole reason I bought this place, has been transformed. Over the weekend, I picked up a soft blue outdoor rug with tassels on the ends, along with several large throw pillows in navy and cream. They're scattered about on the rug, and an overturned basket sits in the center—a makeshift table that holds a bottle of wine and two glasses.

The couple of plants I've had out here since I moved in were dead, so I replaced those too. Two large pine-tree-shaped shrubs sit in gold pots and are decorated with white twinkle lights. The city lights in the distance and the soft hum of the distant traffic below add character. It's cozy and quiet up here, but there's no forgetting we're in the middle of New York City. It lends a certain ambience that's one of a kind. I like it.

I didn't trust myself to make something elaborate, but still, the food smells great. Jumbo shrimp sautéed in butter with angel-hair pasta tossed in olive oil and white wine. It's simple, yet elegant. I'm hoping she likes it. I never thought to ask if she likes seafood. If she doesn't, we can always order pizza.

Pleased, I head into my bathroom, wanting to wash my hands and change my shirt before she arrives. I toss the T-shirt I was wearing into the laundry basket and check my appearance in the mirror. I have no expectations for tonight, but there's no denying I've put more effort into this non-date than I ever put into a regular date.

After washing my hands, I splash a little cologne onto my jaw, then pull on a light-blue cotton button-down.

Even though I've forbidden myself from falling for Camryn, I'm excited to see her tonight. Unhealthy as it may be, I'm becoming attached to seeing her smile, getting a rise out of her, and spending time with her.

Strange as it sounds, I'm coming to look forward to her presence in my life. I didn't realize it until now, but I've been living a lonely existence until she happened into my life. Nights out with bright lights and fast women have been replaced by nights in with one very hard-to-get woman. An interesting fucking turn in events is what it is.

As I check on things in the kitchen one last time, I can't help but recall Camryn's phone call asking about my dating history. Rebecca and I dated for eight months last year, if you can even call it that. Our only connection was work. She's an associate attorney in family law at the firm I work at, and a few nights a week, we got together at her place or mine.

But she wasn't really a girlfriend. A couple of fuck sessions a week, ordering takeout while we sat on my couch with our laptops poring over depositions, wasn't a relationship, wasn't the companionship I crave deep down. She was just filling the empty space for a time, but that ran its course. She still calls every now and then, but the idea of spending time with her just doesn't excite me anymore.

Ever since my mum got sick and my dad buggered off, I've felt more alone than I'd like to let on. Other than a few one-night stands here and there to take the edge off, I haven't had anyone close to me in a long time. I'm not the world's biggest manwhore like people say I am. Of course I enjoy female company, but that's not all that my life's about. I've convinced myself true love only exists in fairy tales, but that doesn't mean I'm immune to female charm. Of course I want a woman in my life.

And what Camryn has to offer is exactly what I've been missing. Easy companionship without any of the weird guessing games, intelligent conversation with a woman, someone who keeps me on my toes.

Unsure what to make of that revelation, I'm pulled away from the kitchen by my ringing phone. The number shows that it's my uncle Charles. I answer it immediately as the overwhelming feeling that something is wrong stirs in my gut.

"Yes?"

"Sterling? It's Charles."

"Has something happened?"

"Yes. I've been trying to reach you for the last hour and a half."

I realize I've been cleaning and cooking, preparing for my date, and feel a sharp and immediate pang of guilt. "What's going on?"

"It's your mum. She suffered a bad episode tonight."

My intention was to go and visit her earlier when I left work, but traffic had been brutal so I abandoned my trip, opting instead to come home and prepare for tonight.

"What happened? Why didn't they call me?"

"They tried. I'm next on the list of contacts."

I look at my phone and realize that I missed a half dozen calls because I was too busy getting ready for my date to be there for my mum.

"Everything is handled. For now."

Fuck. I was distracted, and wasn't there when my

mum needed me.

"Is she okay?" I ask.

Charles lets out a heavy sigh. "She couldn't remember where she was. Tried to harm herself."

My vision blurs and I see red. "What?" I roar. "Is she okay?" Tearing one hand through my hair, I wait in agony for him to answer.

"For now. They had to sedate her, and she's resting in her room."

Mum hasn't had an episode like that in over a year. The doctor's warnings about her medicine losing its effectiveness over time ring in my head. All the more reason why I need to get her the best care money can buy. But the cost of her medicines alone each month is twice my mortgage. I've done the best I can, but it's time to do better.

Charles releases a deep sigh. "I'm telling you, you've got to get her out of that place. You've got to get this inheritance. How's the process coming? You need to be married. There's no other way."

"I know, okay? I'm working on it. Camryn's helping me. She's been great."

Charles releases a sharp exhale. "Don't go falling for the help. She's a pretty face, but don't lose focus. Your mum is counting on you, Sterling."

"I know, all right?" Anger flares inside me, making me resentful that Charles called Camryn a pretty face. She's so much more than that.

The sinking feeling in my chest balloons, and I force a breath into my lungs. "I can be there in forty minutes. Forty-five, tops."

"There's no need, Sterling. She's sleeping now. She'll sleep through the night with the dosage they gave her. Why don't you just go over in the morning?"

"Okay." I hang up, fighting the urge to punch something.

There's no playbook for how to handle it when your loved one's health begins to fade. I'm losing her piece by piece, and I fucking hate it.

I wander out onto the balcony where the romantic

scene seems to mock me. Looking out onto the maze of streets below, I know I shouldn't be here about to wine and dine a woman like Camryn. I should be with my mum, who needs me. I should stick to the fucking plan and do everything in my power to make sure I get that inheritance check, just like my uncle said.

It's time to grow up and stop believing in silly fantasies that won't get me anywhere.

Chapter Thirteen

Camryn

I arrive at Sterling's building at exactly seven with a smile on my lips.

I spent a ridiculous amount of time getting ready for this non-date/hang-out session tonight. After leaving work early, I rushed home to shower and redo my makeup. Now I'm dressed in a pair of well-worn jeans, and since the fall air is cool enough to warrant it, my favorite deep V-neck ivory cashmere sweater with my secret weapon underneath—my lace push-up bra in the softest cream silk. Once I added some layered gold necklaces, I was set. I felt pretty without being overdone.

The building's doorman asks for my name and ushers me inside like he was expecting me. I'm instructed to take the elevator to the tenth floor, and go to unit 1001.

Taking a deep breath, I step onto the elevator and

punch the button for the tenth floor. I have no idea what hanging out with Sterling will involve, but I'm nearly giddy with anticipation. I stop at his door and knock twice, my mouth already twitching with a smile.

After waiting about a minute with no answer, I press my ear to the door. It's quiet inside, no sounds of music, no footsteps, so I knock again.

And wait, my smile fading.

Still nothing.

I twist the doorknob, and finding it unlocked, let myself inside.

Sterling's place is compact, but modern and classy. It suits him. After a quick glance around the living space, I spot him on the balcony outside, just beyond the glass doors at the far end of the living room. He's facing away from me, his hands gripping the railing, his head bowed.

My smile from moments ago is gone. Seeing him like this—looking distraught—brings the reality of our situation crashing back.

Sterling suddenly turns and we lock eyes. A thousand emotions are revealed in his eyes, but mostly there's anger. There's also a sadness in his gaze that I've never seen. It's haunting.

I swallow a lump in my throat, wondering what's going on.

"Sterling?" I ask, slowly approaching the balcony.

It's beautiful—plush pillows and twinkling lights, and a chilled bottle of white wine all nestled together in a romantic picnic for two.

He lets out a heavy sigh and runs one hand through his hair.

"This is beautiful," I say since he hasn't spoken, hasn't even moved from the spot where he's rooted, and his stony silence is killing me. "Are you okay?"

"Just fine," he says curtly, his gaze looking past me.

He doesn't seem fine. He seems off. Why go through all the effort if he's just going to act sullen and withdrawn?

And what could have possibly changed in the

twenty-four hours since we last spoke on the phone? He seemed so excited—like he hadn't a care in the world. Now it seems he doesn't want me here.

"If this is a bad time, if tonight doesn't work . . ." I trail off, my voice suddenly shaky.

"The meal's already prepared." He brushes past me, headed toward the kitchen.

Unsure what to do, I follow behind him.

He's acting like an asshole, and I suddenly feel so stupid for getting all done up tonight. I'm not going to stand around and embarrass myself by begging for his attention.

"You know what? Never mind. This was a bad idea, anyway. I'll see myself out." I turn and head for the front door, anger and rejection dueling inside me.

It takes all of three seconds before Sterling's long strides catch him up to me by the door. His grip around my wrist stops me. "Wait."

I turn and face him. I'm halfway between wanting to flee and staying to hear his explanation.

He releases a heavy exhale. "I received a phone call just before you arrived."

With him so near, the combination of his clean soap and his spicy cologne intoxicates me. Memories of our intimate dinner rush back. But apparently tonight is not meant to be a repeat. Waiting to see what he'll say next, I inhale and hold my breath.

When he doesn't continue, I ask, "Is everything okay?"

"Yeah," he says, recovering quickly. "It was just my uncle Charles. There's some family stuff going on, and he was reminding me of the importance of this inheritance."

"I see."

Looking down at my feet, encased in the cutest pair of brown suede high-heeled boots I own, I suddenly feel like an imposter. All the optimism I had vanishes. This can't work.

"I should go."

Sterling's warm palm comes to rest on my cheek,

and my protest dies on my lips. The conflicted look in his eyes grips something deep inside me. The part of me that believes in true love and happily-ever-afters wants this spark between us to be real, but how can it when he's destined to marry someone else in a matter of months?

He slides his thumb along my jaw, and in that moment, the only thing I'm sure of is that he wants to kiss me, and if he does, I will totally let him.

Chapter Fourteen

I'm seconds away from ruining the evening with my foul mood, but it's hard not to when the call from Charles put everything into shining clarity. My mood plummeted with the gravity of the entire situation I've found myself in, and then it was all I could focus on.

It may sound cliché, but my mum is my whole world. She's the one who stood by my side when I was an unruly, spite-filled teenager who'd just been dropped into a strange new school in a brand-new country. I didn't understand the customs, didn't understand the culture. And worse, I didn't have any friends to take away the boredom and dark pit of juvenile hell I'd found myself wallowing in.

Mum stood up for me, helped get me through. I didn't understand why I couldn't call someone a cunt, or why everyone giggled behind their hand when I said *bloody*. But Mum was there. As an only child, I was her whole world, and now that she has no one else, it's up to me to fight for her.

Eventually I met Noah and got along fine, but those first months were hard.

As I grew, I always stayed close to her. And then somewhere during the process of becoming a divorce attorney and watching my own parents' seemingly stable marriage crumble, I lost it. I lost sight of the meaning of a deep relationship between two people, didn't know why in the world anyone would ever want to tie themselves to another person for all of eternity, knowing the odds of it ending badly were so high.

Because of all of that baggage, I've been living a lonely life. Maybe it's the fact that my best friend has now settled down and has a baby on the way, but I'm starting to look at Camryn in a whole new light.

There's no way this can possibly work out well, so I don't know why I'm even trying. But when Camryn showed up tonight looking stunning, she took my breath away, and then was ready to leave before I've even spoken three words to her. I know I can't stand by and let that happen.

I might have a mess of baggage to deal with, but I'm not about to let her walk away. The urge to pull her into my arms and hold her there is much too strong. I stroke her jaw, fighting with myself not to kiss her, and she looks up at me with huge green eyes.

"Don't leave," I whisper.

She draws a slow, shaky breath, still watching me with wide eyes as I touch her.

This just feels right. And for the first time in a long time, I feel good. I don't want that feeling to end.

I'm still touching her, still caressing her milky-soft skin, and she's still letting me. It's a step in the right direction.

"I was a dick. I'm sorry."

A weak smile is her only response.

"Come on; you can do better than that, love."

Her shaky smile grows, and her rigid posture relaxes just a fraction more. "I wasn't sure what to think when I got here. You seemed pissed off."

"Just a bit of bad news, but I'll get it straightened in the morning. I'm sorry. Will you please stay?"

She nods, and I let my hand slip down from her jaw to the column of her graceful neck, her shoulder, enjoying the brush of soft cashmere against my fingertips as Camryn wets her lower lip with the tip of her tongue. The movement is so quick, but it doesn't stop the erotic images of her mouth on mine, moving over my cock, from taking over. She has a beautiful mouth. And when she's not using it to be sassy, those plump lips are just begging to be kissed.

My hand slides lower until it comes to rest on her lower back. The movement thrusts her chest forward slightly, and her firm breasts graze my chest. She responds with a tiny shiver.

My cock instantly goes hard at the crackling electricity between us. One small touch has never gotten me so ready, so quickly. But the strong suspicion that we'd have explosive chemistry in the bedroom isn't something I can let myself think about right now. Wanting to devour her, to taste her lips and hear her whimpers of desire, I force myself to pull away from the soft curves of her body, her huge, hungry eyes and damp lips.

"Come. Join me," I say, taking her hand.

Camryn nods, and I lead her out onto the balcony.

"Does it always look like this out here?" she asks as we step outside.

"I might have spruced her up a bit," I lie. I spent a solid hour giving this place a total makeover.

Camryn takes a seat on one of the pillows, and I do the same across from her.

I pour us each a glass of wine as we settle in. I watch Camryn take in the view surrounding us. The towering buildings glitter in the distance, and a gentle breeze lifts a stray strand of her hair.

Even though being her with her feels amazing, the dark shadow clouding all of this isn't far from my thoughts.

"If this is how you plan a simple date on a Wednesday evening, I don't think we'll have any trouble getting you married off," Camryn jokes.

I inhale, my jaw ticking. *Right, that's the plan.* "Enjoy your wine. Let me put the finishing touches on dinner."

I excuse myself into the kitchen where I remove our still-warm plates from the oven, and try to push aside the drama fighting for space in my brain.

Just chill, mate. One step at a time.

I deliver Camryn's plate in front of her, along with a cloth napkin and silverware.

"Wow. I'm impressed," she says, surveying the food.

"I hope shellfish is okay."

"Absolutely. This looks amazing."

After I take my spot across from her, we both dig in.

The evening air is crisp, and I settle a woolly throw blanket over her lap. "Are you too cold? We can go inside, if you prefer."

Shaking her head, she tugs the blanket around her. "It's perfect out here," she says, then takes a bite of pasta.

Neither of us seems to want to discuss the elephant in the room, the entire reason we're working together—my upcoming nuptials. So we make small talk and stick to safe topics.

When we're through with dinner, I stack our plates and set them aside, then bring out the chocolate truffles I purchased today and set them on top of the overturned basket.

"Cheers." She touches her chocolate to mine, then pops it in her mouth.

"So, Camryn Palmer. Tell me, what is it that you're looking for?"

She chews and swallows, taking her time savoring the bittersweet chocolate with caramel. "Ultimately, I'm looking for my lobster."

My brows dart up at her unexpected response. "Your lobster?"

She laughs, a short, sharp chuckle that endears her to me even more. "It's probably just a stupid myth, but haven't you ever heard that lobsters mate for life?"

I shake my head. "I think someone fed you a load of shit there, love."

"Oh, shush. Let me have my fantasies."

"Fine." I grin, amused that she's looking for her lobster. "Carry on."

"I'm looking for my forever. Someone to grow old with."

Her dreamy smile quickly fades, and her expression turns to panic. "Oh God, I just told you that I'm looking for commitment. Feel free to run the other way now. Climb down the trellis if you need to."

"You didn't say *I* had to give you a commitment, you simply communicated what *you* were looking for," I say, correcting her. "And a woman knowing what she wants has been, and will always be, quite sexy."

She pulls her bottom lip between her teeth as naughty thoughts flash through my brain.

"I just want to keep this casual," she says. "It'd be foolish to get wrapped up when we have so much going on."

"Yes, of course. Casual would be best," I say.

Camryn takes another sip of her wine. "Can I ask what was bothering you when I got here?"

Fighting through the tightness in my chest, I make the decision to let Camryn in. And while I'm not ready to share everything, I know she deserves to know. It's something I never got around to telling Rebecca, even after eight months together.

Clearing my throat, I say, "My mum's been in poor health lately. It's been tough. And my uncle Charles is just worried, is all."

"I'm sorry," she offers, her voice soft. "I didn't know."

Nodding, I take another sip of wine. I haven't opened up and told anyone about the seriousness of it, but the tender look in Camryn's eyes makes me want to share a little more of myself with her.

"I'm all she has. My father left three years ago."

"I see." Camryn folds her hands in her lap and

looks down at them. "My dad left when I was little."

When she looks up to meet my eyes, I can see the pain and hurt his absence has caused. When someone that vital to your life disappears from it, it leaves a little hole behind. I know that firsthand.

We continue our discussion, moving from topic to topic, and unlike all the other women I've been with, my conversation with Camryn is real. We discuss our goals, more about our families, a little about work. We learn that neither of us has much contact with our dads, something unexpected that we share.

The pain and heartache that goes along with losing your dad isn't something I'd wish on anyone, and the sadness lurking behind her gaze tells me she wishes this was one thing we didn't have in common too.

"Let's have another glass of wine," I suggest.

"I'm game if you are."

Chapter Fifteen

Camryn

Tonight has been more than I could have ever imagined. Anyone looking at my life from the outside may think I have it all. A great career? *Check*. A small, but close-knit group of girlfriends? *Check*.

But my reality is much different. I crave a true connection, a partner in life, someone who gets me and accepts me for who I am. My ex was none of those, and I fooled myself into believing I was having fun—living it up in my twenties with a sexy fling. But deep inside, I yearned for more.

And tonight, Sterling has unknowingly opened a huge gaping wound inside me. He's made me feel special, planned something just for me. Showed me what it was like to spend an evening with a man interested in conversation just for the sake of getting to know me. I fear I'll never be the same.

I haven't dated, haven't been out with anyone since

David the Douche, and honestly, I've all but given up hope that good men actually exist. But if men like Sterling Quinn really do exist, then maybe the hunt for my lobster isn't totally in vain. I still can't believe I told him that. But he was so gracious and sweet about it, so I don't regret it.

We've finished dinner and dessert, and now we're lounging on the pillows outside, drinking a second glass of wine. My heart feels so full and conflicted, I've grown quiet in the past few minutes.

"You asked about my past." Sterling looks out on the passing traffic below as he says this.

I've barely noticed the quiet hum and occasional car horn in the background, as we've been deep in conversation much of the night. Studying his profile, his square jawline peppered with dark stubble, his strong, straight nose and full lips, it takes me a moment to realize he's waiting for me to respond.

"I was curious, yes."

"I had a girlfriend last year. An attorney where I work. It was convenient."

That pang of jealousy I felt earlier when I wondered about his past flares up again. "I see. And how long did you date her?"

"About eight months."

Longer than I would have guessed. "That sounds serious. And you were monogamous the entire time?"

"Of course I was. But no, it wasn't serious; not in the way you're thinking, at least. There were no I-love-yous exchanged," he adds.

"And she's out of your life completely?"

He rubs the back of his neck. "I still see her at the office occasionally, but we work on different floors. She still calls once in a while, but I've moved on."

It seems like it would be the easier choice to marry someone he was comfortable with and has history with over some stranger, but I'm not going to be the one to point that out to him. He must have his reasons.

"And what about you? You were dating someone last year too. David, wasn't it?"

I nod, surprised that Sterling even noticed. Maybe

he silently kept tabs on me like I did on him.

"We broke up about six months ago. He took off." *With my heart, my wallet, and my good credit score.*

"And there's been no one since then?" Sterling asks.

I shake my head. "I haven't had the slightest interest in dating." *Until you.*

"Same here," he says.

"But now you have to get married."

"Seems that way." He rubs the back of his neck again, which I'm coming to recognize as something he does when he's anxious.

"Why are you doing this, really? You're a successful attorney. I'm sure you make a comfortable living."

He lets out a deep sigh. "Come inside with me."

We move inside, carrying the stacks of dishes and our wineglasses. We set the dishes in the kitchen and take our glasses to the couch.

His living room is masculine, yet inviting. A navy

sofa in tweed fabric sits facing the large windows, and a leather armchair and small table made of steel round out the other side of the room. His coffee table is a large rustic crate that's been overturned.

We're sitting side by side on the couch when Sterling takes my wineglass from my hand and sets it on the table next to his.

He's quiet, contemplative, and I wonder what he's thinking about.

I realize it in that moment—we're all struggling to find something true. True affection. True intimacy. True love. A shot at something real in this life. And Sterling and I share that desire. He might deny it, might say that he's jaded on the idea of marriage and that he's doing this for the money, but I can see it when I look into his eyes, can feel it when he smiles at me. He wants something true as badly as I do. He needs it, maybe even more than I do.

"I know this probably seems strange to you, me going through with this cocked-up plan to marry."

I swallow and shake my head. I won't judge him;

there's a lot of freaking money on the line.

"But you have to trust me that I have my reasons. It's not all about the money. Well, it sort of is." He rubs the back of his neck again. "I just need this to work."

I take his hand. "You don't have to explain anything to me. I told you I'll help, and I meant it." A giggle forces its way up my throat. "Just consider tonight me testing your ability to woo a woman."

His smile is amused. "And did I woo you, Miss Palmer?" He's still holding my hand, and when he strokes the back of it with his thumb, tingles of awareness spiral through me.

I'm practically dizzy with the electricity that's been humming between us all evening. He's intoxicatingly attractive, and the lines between professionalism and pleasure have become irrevocably blurred. There should be miles between work friends and fuck buddies, but with Sterling this close, with his subtle, spicy cologne and his deep blue eyes gazing into mine, everything is fuzzy.

"You get an A-plus in the wooing department,

Mr. Quinn," I whisper as Sterling draws near.

"We should probably test out how I kiss. You know, for research purposes," he murmurs.

A warm shudder passes through me. *Dear God, could he get any sexier? If he suggested I test out how he fucked, would I even have the strength to say no?*

His hands are on my jaw, and he tilts my mouth up to meet his. In that split second, I know I could pull away if I wanted to, but I don't. My eyes drift closed just as his warm, full lips press softly against mine. When he sucks lightly on my bottom lip, I open to him. Then, so slowly it makes me ache, he brushes his tongue against mine.

Holy shit.

The.

Man.

Can.

Kiss.

In fact, every kiss I've had since my first in eighth

grade pales in comparison.

Tender. Sensual. Soft. Urgent. His kiss is all of those things at once. And more.

He holds my jaw with one hand while the other trails down the front of my deep V-neck sweater. Careful to avoid my breasts, which ache for his touch, he lightly trails his fingertips along the line of exposed cleavage, leaving warmth tingling in his wake. My entire body silently pleads for more.

When he pulls away, he does so only a few inches, and rests his forehead against mine. "Fuck, you taste good."

Everything inside me clenches. Even the way this man curses is hot.

Pulling back a fraction more, Sterling focuses his eyes on mine. His are dark, glazed over with hot lust, and it makes me want him even more, knowing I affect him as much as he does me.

With a tiny groan at the back of his throat, he pulls back to study me. Swiping his thumb across my lower lip, he releases a pained exhale. He doesn't ask how the kiss was, or tease me to see if he passed the test. We both know that kiss was utterly perfect. Intense. It was the real thing. So real, it's a little scary. Some people just click—their chemistry or pheromones or something. I know I could easily fall for him, and given the direction his life's headed, I can't let that happen.

"We should stop before we do something we can't take back," he says.

"Or something we'll regret in the morning."

I rise from the couch while Sterling does the same. The obvious strain at the front of his jeans is impossible not to notice. *Holy erection!*

He clears his throat and leads me toward the door.

We stand there, our breathing ragged as though we've just run an Olympic race, not quite ready to say good night.

Feeling brazen, this time I'm the one lifting up on my toes to press my lips against his. It's meant to be a chaste kiss good-bye, but that's all it takes for Sterling's control to snap. His hands thread through the hair at the back of my neck as he tilts my mouth to his. He explores my mouth with deep, drugging kisses as I writhe against him, desperate for more.

The connection we shared tonight was more than physical. But nothing could have prepared me for this. The grinding of his hips against mine, the rigid length of his massive erection pressing *right there*. I want more.

Growing need outweighs all common sense. Hooking one leg around his waist, I pull us closer. He drags his hands up my sides, his touches changing from innocent to seductive as he palms my breasts, massaging them, grazing my pebbled nipples with his thumbs.

I suck in a breath at the sudden wash of heat rushing through me.

Overcome with lust, I reach down to grip the firm bulge of his erection. Even covered in denim, it's impressive, warm and solid in my palm.

With a grunt, he swears under his breath, pressing us even closer so that his hands are now on my ass and his thigh is pressed between my legs.

Ripping my mouth from his, I suck in a deep breath. I feel as though I've been underwater, deprived of oxygen for too long. My heart is hammering, and I'm dizzy and flushed.

"I'd better go." My voice comes out so soft, and I realize it's because I haven't spoken a single word since that kiss that tipped my world upside down.

He opens the door for me and leans against the frame while I slip my purse over one shoulder. "Thank you for coming over."

"I had fun," I whisper, my lips damp and swollen from his onslaught of hungry kisses.

"We should hang out again." He smiles.

I nod, unsure how in the world I'll be able to hang out with him again without things between us turning heated.

His expression changes, and I see something dark pass through his gaze. "Are you sure about this?"

I shrug. "Someone's going to have to keep an eye this shit show."

He chuckles and gives me a brief hug before releasing me. "Night, Camryn," he murmurs.

When I make it downstairs, the friendly doorman has a cab waiting for me.

"Good evening, miss," he calls as I slip inside.

Miss.

The word only serves to remind me that some other girl is soon going to be *Mrs.* Sterling Quinn. The thought is sobering.

Chapter Sixteen

Sterling

As I stand here cleaning the dishes, I'm in shock at how well tonight went. I went out on a limb, given that I never plan dates, and Camryn isn't even someone I'm supposed to be dating, but that was incredible. That kiss. The conversation. How much she affected me. Her soft, tempting curves, the way she shivered when I fondled her gorgeous breasts.

I wanted more with her, to explore her body and make her cry out in pleasure. I wanted to watch her come on my tongue, my fingers, my cock. I get half-hard again just picturing it. Her head thrown back in ecstasy, her honey-colored hair spread across my pillow, those perfect pink lips crying out my name.

But I settled for her sweet, tender kisses because there's one thing I'm certain of. When we make love, it will damn sure be on a bed where I can take my time with her. Camryn deserves intimacy and someone who'll look after her needs properly.

I wonder if she'd like it slow and tender—leisurely lovemaking with plenty of soft kisses. Or hard and fast, my hips driving my cock deep inside her over and over again. Maybe she likes a bit of both . . .

Fuck. Many more erotic daydreams like that and I'll be tossing off to thoughts of her for the third time this week.

That shit about her finding her lobster—I smile when I think of it. Behind her tough persona, she's actually quite a softy. A romantic. The basic human need for closeness has never felt so real. I've spent the past years pushing all of it from my brain, but now, confronted with someone who challenges all my preconceived notions, I'm awestruck.

My hands pause in the dishwater.

Fuck.

That was my one rule. I promised myself that under no circumstances would I fall for her.

But I can already feel it happening.

This won't end well if real feelings get involved.

Camryn will end up hurt, and I'll be the arsehole who broke her heart. My uncle's words from earlier tonight ring in my ears.

Pissed off at myself for possibly fucking up the one positive thing in my life right now, my friendship with Camryn, I throw the dishtowel onto the counter. I need to stay focused. And tonight with her, I've been anything but. I was ready to call off the entire wedding charade, just for a chance to sink into her warm body.

Knowing I won't be able to sleep until I blow off some steam, I figure a long drive out to New Jersey should do the trick. I can check on my mum too, and that always helps put my mind at ease. I grab my keys and stalk out into the night.

• • •

I spent the night curled up on the small waiting-room couch, and now I'm sitting in the rocking chair beside my mum's bed.

We're sharing a cup of tea, and my somber mood from last night has disappeared somewhat. Being here with her, reminding myself of my purpose, all of those things seem to help.

Mum has a bandage on her arm where scratch marks from last night lay underneath. She looks around, her brows knitting together as she takes in the room around us.

Given her bewildered expression, I think she's about to ask where we are, which she has countless times. Most times she remembers that she lives here now for treatment, and that she's sick. But other times, it falls on me to break the devastating news to her like it's the first time she's heard it.

"Where's your dad?" she asks.

I set down my tea and take a deep breath.

Explaining to my dear mum for the third time this month that my father is gone, that he pissed off and left us, isn't something I want to put her through. I simply don't have the strength, and neither does she, I think.

"He's just run out for milk. He'll be back in a few minutes," I lie, the words like sandpaper in my throat.

Mum watches my eyes like she's deciding whether

she should believe me, then gives me a nod. "You're such a good boy, Sterling."

I'm not. Not at all, but I'm trying to be.

Chapter Seventeen

Camryn

"Are you serious? Do I really have to spell this out for you, Camryn?" Anna's eyebrows dart up.

"What?" I'm sitting in a massaging pedicure chair, wedged between my two besties and utterly confused as to what we're talking about.

Before Olivia waddled in, I filled Anna in on what exactly *hanging out* with Sterling had entailed. Well, not *everything*. She can't ever know that I dry-humped his leg at his front door like a dog in heat. Hot shame rushes through me. *So unprofessional.* But she does know we kissed.

"For a girl with a business degree and a successful career, you can be really freaking stupid sometimes," Anna says.

"What in the world is she talking about?" Olivia asks, looking perplexed.

"Not a clue." I submerge my feet into peppermint-scented water that's the perfect temperature—one level below scalding. *Ahh.* Releasing a satisfied sigh, I close my eyes.

"Now, tell me what this nonsense is about."

"Camryn and Sterling hung out last night. At his place," Anna says.

"Hung out?" Olivia asks, her hand absently stroking her belly.

Anna shrugs. "That's what the kids are calling it these days."

"I don't understand," Olivia says. "How's the search coming? Are you finding any good candidates for him to date?"

"Yeah, Camryn, are you?" Anna smiles like she knows all of my secrets.

Fuck. Maybe she does. Maybe she can see straight through me, feel the desire I have for him.

I clear my throat, hoping to sound professional. "Yes, actually. There are a few who look promising so far."

"That's great. Charles Quinn is paying a small fortune for our services, so I don't want to let him down. And of course, Sterling. As crazy as this situation is, he deserves to get that inheritance."

I nod solemnly. She's absolutely right.

"Since you have some great candidates all lined up, I take it he'll be going on dates soon?" Anna asks, probing.

"Absolutely."

I grit my teeth. What the hell is with Anna? She's the one who encouraged me to go out with Sterling in the first place, and now she's acting like I've done something wrong?

"That's good to hear." Olivia rises from her chair, slipping her swollen feet into the pink foam sandals. "I have to pee *again*," she says with a groan.

Once Olivia's out of earshot, Anna turns to face me. "What's going on with you and Sterling?" she hisses. "The truth."

"What do you mean? I told you already. We hung out. It was . . . nice. And we might have kissed at the end." I can't look her in the eye as I say that last part. *She's right. I am stupid.*

Anna rolls her eyes. "Listen, I was all for hooking up with the hottie British walking aphrodisiac, but that was before I realized that you actually liked him." Anna lets out a heavy sigh. "If you fall for him, if real feelings get involved, and let's face it, they will, because I know you, Cam," she says, giving me a side-eyed look, "it's not going to end well. It can't."

"It's fine, Anna. I'm fine."

"You're a smart girl, and I love you. But don't be stupid enough to get involved with him. You said so yourself; he's a manwhore."

I inhale and hold my tongue as Olivia waddles back from the bathroom.

My mood has turned, and what was supposed to be a fun girls' night out has turned into a counseling session. I don't even want to be here anymore. If I could pull my feet out of this tub and march out of here right now, I would.

But the thing is, Anna's right. And she's only trying to protect me. So instead of making a dramatic exit, I bite my tongue and try to enjoy myself as the pedicurist rubs warm oil onto my feet. Which, honestly, isn't difficult to do.

My monthly pedicure outing with my girlfriends is one of my favorite days. This is my happy place. Perched on our thrones, we transition to safer topics like baby names and bucket list items, and who's banging whom at the office.

I watch as my toes are painted cherry red, my earlier discomfort slipping away.

"Noah and I are wanting to try that fancy Italian place, La Brasso, before the baby comes, but there's a three-month waiting list for reservations."

Anna smirks, and if my feet weren't otherwise occupied, I would kick her. But deciding I don't want to conceal something from Olivia, I speak up.

"Sterling and I went there last weekend," I manage to say.

"No kidding?" she asks. "Wow. Wonder how he got you guys in." She rubs her chin, seemingly more concerned about how to score a reservation than the fact that I was there with her husband's best friend.

I breathe a sigh of relief as we finish up. Maybe Anna's wrong. Maybe this isn't the worst thing in the world.

Once we're done, we head to the front of the spa to pay. Anna's busy swiping her credit card and making small talk with the cashier when Olivia turns to face me.

"Promise me one thing," she says, her face solemn.

My best guess is that she's going to make me swear not to let anyone take any of those horrible hospital-bed pictures after you've just had a baby and your vagina is still hanging out.

"Of course. Anything."

She grips my shoulders, looking deep into my eyes. "Promise me you won't fall for Sterling."

My mouth goes dry, and I find myself nodding. "Of course," I mutter, but it already feels like a lie.

Chapter Eighteen

Camryn

I'm not normally one to succumb to peer pressure, but in this instance, I crumbled faster than a cookie at snack time. When Anna and Olivia asked me last night about lining up a date for Sterling, at first I scoffed at the idea, but the stack of printouts on my desk have been calling my name.

I leaf through the pile again. Smiling faces of hopeful women stare back at me, each with the secret desire to become Mrs. Sterling Quinn. I want to shove these into the back of a drawer, or better yet, the recycle bin, but instead I select one at random from the pile.

Meredith Aimes.

She's got long dark hair that hangs in a sleek curtain down her back, and a regal, classy look. She's beauty-queen pretty. Glancing over her profile, I discover she's a former competitive swimmer, currently a teacher at a special-education school, and volunteers in her free time at an animal shelter.

Nope. That's a hard pass. I set her profile aside. I might be willing to set him up, but not with someone who's freaking perfect.

I grab another three sheets from the stack and reject all three. A sweet nanny who loves watching football. A chef with a passion for public service. A gymnast who visits her sick grandma every Sunday after church.

Lifting another, I swallow a curse. A brown-eyed temptress with tits out to there. *Fuck!* Those things are magnificent. They put my B-cups to shame. Sterling doesn't need to see these. Fat chance of that happening when I shove her photo straight into the garbage.

Shit. What is up with all these Miss Perfects?

Annoyed, I grab one more.

Bianca Tetherdine. Blond. Perky. A college student, barely twenty-one.

I roll my eyes. *Fine.*

This will work. She's cute, so he won't suspect

anything. It's not like I can send him off with someone fugly. But I also doubt they'll have anything in common.

I text Sterling to ask if he's free this weekend, and once he confirms he is, I get everything all set up. Bianca's free to meet for a drink tomorrow night. I confirm the time and place with her, then text Sterling again.

> *CAMRYN: I've set you up on a date tomorrow. You're meeting Bianca at eight at Lucky's Tavern.*

I expect a text back. Part of me wants to hear him complain about the idea, so I can pat myself on the back for this little experiment, feeling content that he'd prefer to spend his time with me.

But when a text doesn't arrive, I fear perhaps this is what he's been waiting for all along. This is my job, what I'm supposed to be doing.

Sterling obviously realizes that, and it's time I did too. Anna was right all along.

With a heavy heart, I get back to work, intent on pushing all this Sterling business from my brain.

Hours later, I'm lost in work when a shriek from the office next door steals my attention.

"What was that?" I ask Anna.

"Not a clue. Come on."

I push out of my chair and follow her. Normally, I'm not one for office gossip, but I could use a little distraction from my lackluster day.

Next door to our shared office is an open space containing six desks for a team of graphic designers. While they lack individual offices, the space is bright and open, and is often used as a communal gathering space for those hoping to catch the latest office gossip.

"What's going on?" Anna asks as we stroll up.

Stopping near the workstation where they're all gathered, I see a picture of Sterling on the computer screen. It appears to be a tabloid article. My stomach turns uneasy.

"Just the latest on the gossip site's latest

obsession—Sterling Quinn. He's rumored to be involved in a secret affair, which could jeopardize the whole marriage/inheritance thing."

"W-what do you mean?" Anna asks on my behalf, since I've suddenly found myself speechless.

Leaning against the side of the desk, I force my gaze from the screen and down to a designer, who's apparently got all the inside scoop.

"Spill it, Rocky," I say.

And he does.

"There're pictures with him and some woman kissing in a corridor."

He scrolls down the web page, and I see it in all its glory. Sterling's muscular form wrapped around some tall redhead, their mouths fused together.

Asshole!

Something inside my chest aches, and I feel light-headed. I blink, but the image remains.

"Fuck." I push off the desk and stalk away, utterly

disgusted.

Not only could this jeopardize our working relationship, and the money on the line, but more than that, I trusted him, believed in him, thought we'd made a special connection. Maybe as friends; maybe as more.

Anna follows me back to our office. "Are you okay?" she asks, closing the door behind us.

Nausea rolls through me as I drop into my office chair. "A woman came forward saying she spent the night with him recently. How do you think I'm doing?"

Anna sighs softly, lowering herself into the chair across from me. "Maybe it's for the best. I mean, this whole project was crazy. Very nineteenth century, the idea of an arranged marriage. And then with things getting complicated between the two of you? This was a recipe for disaster from the onset. You see that, don't you?"

I never imagined Sterling and I would have a connection like that. Of course, I think he's attractive; even a blind nun could see that. I figured that maybe there would be some mild innuendo thrown around, some flirting, but I never accounted for the deeper attraction that sizzles below the surface.

All the more reason to set him up for a date this weekend. It's time to move on, and sticking with the original plan has never sounded better. Get Sterling successfully married off, and then collect my bonus.

"I'm just pissed that he lied to me," I grumble.

"Amen, sister," Anna says, nodding.

Trying to immerse myself in work, I begin reviewing the campaign that Anna spent much of this week working on. She's really been a godsend. She's helped with my workload since she started last week, and every day promptly at two, she runs down to the coffee shop downstairs and returns with two iced lattes. I think that's easily my favorite part.

"I think we deserve a special treat today," Anna announces, rising from her desk at ten to two.

"Agreed." Today has been stupid. "What are you thinking?"

She lifts her purse from the back of her chair and

winks at me. "It's a surprise. Be back in ten."

I chuckle to myself and watch her go.

I'm typing away, lost in my work, when just a few minutes later, I hear footsteps outside my office door. For a second, I think it's Anna, that maybe she forgot her wallet. But that's not right, because I saw her grab her purse. When I look up, my breath catches.

It's Sterling.

Dressed in a pair of dark jeans and a crisp white button-down shirt with a gray tweed overcoat, he's so deliciously British, my chest aches. His hair is pushed up in the front, and he's sporting a five o'clock shadow. He looks devastatingly handsome, and that simple fact pisses me off.

I can't let my body react to his. *Focus, Camryn.*

I continue typing out the summary I was working on, trying not to let his masculine, spicy cologne totally fucking derail me.

"Did you need something?"

He slides into the guest chair in front of my desk.

"Are you okay?" His tone is unusually hollow.

Distracted, I abandon my e-mail for good and fold my hands in front of me. "Just fucking dandy. Why do you ask?"

He swallows, his Adam's apple bobbing in his throat, and he leans forward, gripping the edge of my desk. "Because my name is being splashed all over the tabloids saying I've been carrying on with another woman, and then I get a text from you saying you've set me up on a date."

I tilt my head to the side, relieving some of the pressure building at the base of my neck. I can feel a massive headache coming on. So he did receive my text, but rather than responding to it like a normal human, he decided to confront me in person.

"I'm just trying to do my job, Sterling. And now I have a media circus to clean up on top of it, thanks to your . . . *indiscretions.*"

"For fuck's sake, Camryn, that's what I came here to tell you. That story is fabricated."

I let out a sharp, humorless laugh. "They have

pictures of you with her!" My voice comes out sounding wild, hurt.

Sterling rises to his feet and closes the door to my office, apparently not wanting anyone to overhear our conversation. Even if I am pissed at him, I appreciate the gesture. I don't need my office neighbors to hear me go off the rails, to know how emotionally invested I've become in my *job*.

Taking a deep breath, I try to rein in my reaction to him showing up here.

Sterling comes around the side of my desk, leaning down to face me so we're eye to eye. My mouth goes dry the second his deep blue eyes latch onto mine.

"Will you please just listen to me," he pleads. "I haven't lied to you yet, and if you understood the first thing about me, it's that I never will."

"I'm all ears. I'd love to hear you explain when you had the time to go out with that woman between taking me out on Saturday night, and then spending Wednesday evening with you too. Quite a voracious appetite you have. I underestimated you."

"The story is bullshit. Those pictures are of me and my ex from months ago."

I pause, staring at him, trying to understand how I can possibly trust him again. I'm way more involved that I should be, in way over my head. The smart thing to do would be to cut my losses and move on.

"Look at the freaking picture, Camryn." He grabs a folded-up printout of the story from his back pocket and stabs at it with his finger. "We're dressed in T-shirts. Do you really think that's recent?"

God, he's right. I'm a PR executive, and if I've learned one thing working in this field, it's not to believe the tabloids. The way the media can spin those stories, you're often left with only the tiniest kernel of truth. It's fall in New York. Definitely not T-shirt weather.

I take a deep breath and shake my head. "Is that your ex?"

"Rebecca, yeah."

The mental image of them kissing is singed into my brain. Shrugging my shoulders, I try to shake it off, but it's no use. *Christ, when did this get so complicated?*

"I'm sorry," he says. "Are you okay?"

I nod, fighting with myself to let it go. "It'll be fine."

"I really have to do this, don't I?" he asks with a smirk.

"Marry? Only if you want to."

The tick in his jaw tells me the idea is a foreign one. He leaves the perch at the side of my desk and returns to the seat across from me.

"Are you all right?" he asks.

"What do you mean?"

"I wanted to check in on you. Wanted to come in person. I needed to see your eyes, make sure you believed me."

"I do believe you. None of that changes the fact that you still need to go on this date."

He combs his long fingers through the front of his hair. "Fuck me."

I release a heavy sigh. There's no escaping the

reality of our situation. We each have a role to play, a job to do.

"She's a nice girl. Go and have fun."

He makes a noise of frustration and rises to his feet. "I'll go, under one condition."

"Name it." I rise to stand before him. Even though I'm wearing heels, he still towers over me.

"After the date, you meet up with me—"

"I don't think that's a good idea," I say, interrupting him.

"To debrief and discuss how it went," he continues.

Chewing on my lip, I debate the merit of his suggestion. It's actually a pretty decent idea. "Fine. Call me after."

He kisses the back of my hand and disappears.

Anna returns moments later carrying a chocolate cupcake with a mountain of whipped frosting, but I've found my stomach is in knots and my appetite is gone.

Chapter Nineteen

Sterling

I've never been this uninterested in a date before in my life. And I can't figure out why. Bianca is attractive and engaging; so, what in the hell is wrong with her?

She's not Camryn.

It's at this precise moment, over calamari and pints of cold beer, that I understand that I'm truly fucked. If I can't date because I'm falling for my matchmaker, that means I can't marry. And if I don't marry, I don't get my inheritance, which means I can't take care of my mum. Rock, meet hard place.

Nodding along to something Bianca's saying, I stifle a yawn behind my fist.

I want to tell Camryn everything. I want to date her, want to see if it can lead to something real, but if I tell her all of that, I run the risk of scaring her off. I don't know that she wants to be Mrs. Quinn. It's also possible it won't work between us, in which case I'm fucked.

Deciding it's a risk I just can't take, I know what I need to do. Play along with Camryn's plan long enough to get her to fall for me.

Discreetly checking my watch again, I calculate exactly how long until Camryn's in my arms again.

Chapter Twenty

Camryn

I pace my apartment, checking the clock yet again. Sterling and Bianca are an hour into their date, and I'm freaking the fuck out.

In an effort to distract myself, I've tried reading, watching TV, and baking, and I abandoned all three. A bowl of messed-up brownie batter containing salt instead of sugar was dumped into the trash, and I'm now sitting at my dining table with the latest stack of bills and collection letters that I've been avoiding going through.

Leafing through the pile, I try to figure out how I got myself here. I was always so responsible with my money. Having grown up with very little, I knew enough to be careful with what I had.

David the Dick did not. The first time I learned he charged something to my credit card—a set of speakers—we had a major fight. I couldn't understand how someone I'd been dating for only a few months could do something like that behind my back. He swore it would never happen again, and that he'd pay the bill. Of course that never happened, and months later I learned he'd not only charged more to my credit card, but he'd charged items to my Amazon account, using my laptop when I wasn't home. Then he sold all the merchandise and took off with the money. Leaving me in the biggest hole of my life.

My blood pressure rising, I make a tally of all the charges. Just under ten thousand dollars, which will be the exact amount I'll get when I succeed in this crazy project. I have to.

Needing a distraction from the chaos on my dining table, I head into the kitchen to pour myself a glass of red wine. My cheap five-dollar bottle of wine is my weekly splurge. Well, that and the monthly pedicures I haven't been able to give up, mostly just for the girl-time it affords me.

My cell phone rings and I grab it from the counter, giddy and light-headed when I see Sterling's name displayed on the screen. I answer on the first ring.

"Hello?"

"Hello, beautiful." Sterling's warm, silky voice washes over me.

I laugh at his attempt to be smooth. "How did it go, Romeo?"

"Quite well, I think."

He sounds optimistic and cheerful. My stomach twists into a painful knot.

"Where are you?" he asks. "We're still on to debrief, yes?"

Part of me wants to fake the stomach flu or a bout of chicken pox, anything to avoid having to hear about his date—that obviously went well—in all its gory detail. But of course I won't. We agreed to this, I remind myself.

"I'm at home."

"Great. Text me your address and I'll be right over."

"See you soon." I text him my address and then

head to my room to freshen up.

When Sterling arrives fifteen minutes later, I'm ready. I enjoyed my glass of wine while perched on my bathroom counter, touching up my makeup. And now I'm feeling more relaxed and prepared to hear all about his date, or so I tell myself.

He removes his jacket, and I pour him a glass of wine as he surveys my place.

"Great view," he says, wandering over toward the wall of windows with his wineglass in hand.

"Thanks. I've lived here for three years. It's cramped, but that view and the fact that I hate moving have kept me here."

Sterling wanders from the window to the sofa, and sits, patting the seat next to him. There's a hopeful sort of longing in his eyes, and I brace myself for what's about to come out of his mouth.

Lowering myself to the cushion next to him, I take another fortifying sip of wine.

"Did you do anything fun tonight?" he asks.

I shake my head. "If you count binge-watching TV fun, then yes. I had a blast."

He chuckles. "What shows do you like to watch?"

"I'm a teensy bit obsessed with *House Hunters International*. It's silly."

"It's not silly. Not to me, anyway. Would you like to live abroad someday?"

I shake my head. "Not really, but I would love to travel."

"What's stopping you?" He lifts a strand of my hair from my shoulder, rubbing the silky ends between his fingers. It's distractingly sexy to watch him.

"Money, for one. Things are kind of tight right now. Someday, though, I'd love to go to Italy."

"I'll take you to Italy."

I laugh. "You can't just take me to Italy. That's crazy."

"Why is that crazy?"

I pull my hair back into a ponytail, and out of his

grasp. He needs to stop being so sweet and attentive. Things are already confusing between us.

"Don't keep me in suspense any longer. I want to hear about your date. Tell me, are my matchmaking skills superb?"

He takes another sip of wine, his eyes never leaving mine as he swallows. "She was . . . nice."

"*Nice?*" That's all he's going to give me, after I've been sitting here in agony for two hours?

He shrugs. "A bit young for me. But we got along fine."

There's something he's not telling me, and I intend to get it out of him. "So, you'd like to see her again?"

"Let's not get ahead of ourselves." He takes another sip of his wine, then sets down the glass.

"I don't understand." I set my glass beside his. "We have a limited timetable here."

Clearing his throat, he glances to the windows again before meeting my gaze. "Did you ever want something you can't have?"

A wave of lust rolls through me. "Yes." My voice is just a whisper.

Sterling leans in, cupping my jaw as he guides my mouth to his. Hot and hungry is the only way to describe his kiss. His tongue slides against mine, deepening our connection, and in that moment, I'm lost to him.

He is my everything. My unrequited crush. The source of my desire. He's the thing my fantasies are made of.

Sterling makes me wish that happily-ever-afters weren't just for fairy tales. Because to me, he is perfection. All that cocky British swagger wrapped up in one delicious package is hot enough to make panties melt.

Wrapping my arms around his powerful shoulders, I move in closer, kissing him back with every ounce of the hot, fiery passion burning through my veins.

His mouth is hot and demanding, and when he pulls me into his lap so I'm straddling him, I'm powerless to resist. The hard ridge of his cock is nestled right between my legs, and I gasp as the firm, broad tip drives me insane with hot friction.

I squirm in his lap as my rising lust demands attention. The wetness between my legs grows, and for a moment, I'm worried he'll be able to feel it. Then I decide I just don't care. I rock against him as we kiss, savoring each wave of pleasure cresting through me.

He makes me feel alive and desirable. It's addicting.

"Do you have any idea how sexy you are?" he growls.

I chew on my lip, sure that's a rhetorical question.

"The sounds you make, the way you taste. You're so fucking tempting."

I know exactly what he means. Never in my life have I been so tempted to say *fuck it* to my morals and have a dirty night of debauchery. Sadly, I know I'm not the type who can do that without regretting it in the morning. I've always been more of a committed-relationship type of girl. But I think I've been missing out on the casual fun other people my age seemed to enjoy.

"Sterling . . ." I grip his shoulders and push him back. "We need to stop."

As hard as it is, I make myself climb off his lap. At the far end of the couch, I pull my knees to my chest and take a deep breath.

"You're not dating anyone, are you?" he asks.

"I wouldn't be here doing this with you if I was." Pushing my hands into my hair, I release a long exhale. "I shouldn't be doing this, anyway."

He leans closer and rubs his thumb across my lower lip, his expression amused. "I'm sorry."

"No, you're not."

Smiling at me, he chuckles. "You're right. I'm not sorry. There's no denying we have an attraction."

"We can't let ourselves get carried away," I correct him, using my sternest voice. "And I'm serious this time."

"Aye-aye, captain."

His attempt at being funny only endears him to me

more. Because, us keeping our hands to ourselves? The struggle is real.

I excuse myself to the restroom for a few minutes, and when I emerge, I find Sterling standing in front of the windows, looking out at the traffic that never seems to slow.

"Can I ask you something?" I've been wondering about this since we started our special project; I just haven't had the courage to ask until now.

"Sure," he says, turning to face me.

"What are the qualities you're looking for in a wife?"

His gaze moves from mine to the floor. "That's tough to answer. Never thought I'd have a wife. I never wanted to get married."

"But you're still going through with this, right?" I ask, suddenly feeling unsure.

"Of course. I told you, I have my reasons, but I have to go through with this."

I nod. "I remember."

"I suppose the qualities that are important are someone honest. Someone who gets along with my mum. It would help if we had compatibility inside and outside the bedroom." He smirks.

"Yes, that would help."

"I haven't put as much thought into it as I should have. I'm sorry."

I shake my head. "What about Rebecca . . . have you thought about her? You guys already know each other; obviously you did share some common interests."

He clears his throat. "Our shared interests were work and that we both liked fucking."

My eyes widen. Okay, that wasn't what I was expecting to hear. The thought of him with someone else makes my palms sweat, and I get that dizzy feeling that comes right before you get sick.

"I'm sorry." He takes my hand.

"No, I'm sorry. I shouldn't have pried."

We're still learning about each other, feeling out this whole unique situation. But it's moments like this where we share real conversation that I discover more of the man he is underneath.

"I'm no saint. I'm sorry to disappoint you. If you want to walk away now, I totally get it."

I force a sad smile onto my lips. "And miss all the fun? I'm not going anywhere."

"Thank God. I need you if I'm to survive the next six months."

I walk him to the door, then take two steps back so I'm not tempted to contort my body around his muscular one, or steal another mind-blowing kiss.

Sterling releases a sharp exhale, pinching the bridge of his nose. "This is just fucking bollocks. There's someone I genuinely like right now and I have no idea where it might lead, but I have this time bomb ticking in the background, deciding my fate for me. Talk about the worst fucking timing ever."

Butterflies tingle inside my stomach. "Then you should find a way to show her how you feel."

We share an intense moment where his eyes don't

leave mine, and I find myself swaying forward the tiniest bit.

"Show her?"

I nod. "Actions speak louder than words."

"Right." He rubs the back of his neck. "You're absolutely right."

"Night, Sterling," I say as he steps into the hall.

"Night, gorgeous."

I close the door and press my back against it, then immediately sink to the floor. My legs are mush, and the only thing that's going to cool me down is a cold shower.

Chapter Twenty-One

Sterling

After spending the weekend thinking about Camryn, I'm back at work on Monday, and doing my best to throw myself into the cases piling up on my desk. Technically, I practice family law, which means I spend my days drafting prenuptial agreements, and handling divorce proceedings as well as alimony and child custody.

Very rarely, I also handle a personal bankruptcy, or help with an adoption. I've also been asked to speak at conferences about family law or ethics. But ask anyone I work with what I'm known for, it's divorce. The big D is what I've lived and breathed for five years now, and what I've built my reputation and career on.

So color me fucking surprised that the man known for divorce now has to get married.

The irony is not lost on me.

And the craziest part is that I've started to fall for

my matchmaker. I know she's interested in me physically—but she's given me no reason to believe she wants to throw her name into the hat for a shot at becoming Mrs. Sterling Quinn.

Needing a break from the mountain of work on my desk that only seems to mock me, I've asked Noah to meet me for lunch. At ten to noon, I walk over to the restaurant where we're supposed to meet.

"You look like hell, brother. What's up?" Noah asks when he spots me outside the restaurant.

"I've had a lot on my mind," I mutter. "Come on, let's get a table. I'm starving."

We're seated at the sushi bar, where we glance at the menu. Once we place our orders, Noah turns to face me.

"Is everything okay? I've never seen you rattled before."

"That's because I've never been rattled before."

"Getting married is a big deal, man. How's it coming, by the way?"

I make a noncommittal noise in my throat. "Nonexistent so far. I've been on one mediocre date, but Camryn's planning a big event next month where I'll be speed dating my way through all the hopefuls."

"Next month?"

Shit. He's right. It's already the end of the month. "In about three weeks," I say, correcting myself, stunned at how fast this is all happening.

Our food arrives, and I waste no time dosing a piece of spicy tuna roll with wasabi. "Let me ask you a question. What kind of girls are going to go to an event like that, really?"

He tilts his head, considering it. "Good point. Probably only those looking for a bit of the limelight, who want a piece of the fortune. Is that what you mean?"

I nod. "Exactly. My guess is that for every one hundred opportunity-seekers, there will be one genuine girl looking for love. And what are the chances that I'll have a connection with any of them?"

"What are you saying? What do you propose

then?" Noah steals a piece of my eel roll.

"Camryn." I take a sip of tea, waiting for him to answer.

"Shit. You were serious about that before? I thought you were drunk and horny."

"Sadly, no." Horny, yes. She's left me with blue balls twice now, and if I get the opportunity to be alone with her again, it's my life's mission to change that.

"Okay, so you *like her* like her. As in, you want to marry her?"

"Fuck." I set down my chopsticks. "The idea of marriage makes me itchy."

Noah smiles wryly. "You want my advice?"

"'Course I do."

"If you're going to be a bear, be a grizzly," Noah says before munching another bite of shrimp tempura.

What the fuck. Maybe he's hit his head. "Meaning?"

"Go after what you want. Fight dirty. Get it. Make

it happen." Grinning, Noah claps me on the back.

"Be a grizzly, huh?" I smirk. Must be American slang. Stupid as shit, but I think I catch the meaning.

"You've got this." He smiles, nodding. "Are you done with that spicy tuna?"

I push the plate toward him. "Have at it; I'm going to get back to the office. I've got grizzly-esque items to check off my list."

He shakes his head, popping another bite of sushi into his mouth. "Damn British. You make everything sound so fancy and refined."

I toss a couple of bills on the table and head out, my head clearer, my heart fuller. Time to go after what I want, consequences be damned.

I want to text Camryn, *Shield your ovaries, girl. Sterling's about to up the seduction game.* But it won't be any fun giving her advance warning.

As I step inside the office tower's foyer, I spot Rebecca coming off the lift.

Fuck.

I've been dodging her calls for weeks now. This isn't going to be good. I haven't spoken to her since the news broke of my inheritance.

"Ster . . ." She pauses with her cell phone halfway to her ear.

"Hi." I give her an awkward half wave while my gaze darts left, then right, looking for the emergency exit.

"I'll have to call you back," she says into her phone, then drops the thing into her briefcase.

I shove my hands in my pockets as I wait. I know she's pissed.

"Why didn't you just tell me?" Her eyes latch onto mine and then narrow into the shape of slivered almonds.

"About?"

"The inheritance!" she shouts.

I take her elbow and guide her over to the seating area. It's not private, but it's better than standing in the center of the lobby with people all around us.

"I found out about it the day before the news broke. If you can believe it, I was more than a little in shock. I didn't exactly spend the day calling everyone I knew to inform them. The only people I spoke with were my mother and Noah."

She scoffs. "Don't even get me started on that. You two have an unhealthy relationship." Then her gaze softens, and she places one hand against the arm of my suit jacket. "Still, you should have called. I could help you, Ster."

"Listen, Rebecca, I don't mean to be a dick, but what we had has run its course."

She smiles seductively, wetting her lower lip with the tip of her tongue. "It was fun. Even you have to admit that."

I know what she's trying to do. She's trying to be sweet and demure, and make me remember her good qualities.

She's only half right, though. We did have some fun between the sheets, but being married, taking a wife—I need a hell of a lot more than someone fun in bed. In fact, that's just one tiny requirement on my list. All too clear in my memory are the times when she'd rather stare at her phone than me while we were in bed, or that time she threw a fit when I ordered the wrong pizza toppings. What we had wasn't love, wasn't even on the same spectrum as love.

Releasing a heavy sigh, I mentally search for a way to say this that doesn't end with my face getting slapped. "Here's the thing. We were convenient. We leaned on each other while we avoided real relationships."

Her optimism falls, and she takes a step back. "I see. And here I thought what we had was nice. Am I the only one who remembers it fondly?"

I keep my mouth shut, because I think agreeing will only encourage her more. Plus, I'm going to be late for my one o'clock meeting if I don't get back upstairs.

"I'm sorry. I've got to run."

Crossing her arms in front of her chest, she nods. "Good luck."

Once inside my office, I realize I have five minutes before the conference call starts, so I grab the stack of papers from my briefcase that I lifted on Friday night from Camryn's place. I'm sure she'll want to kill me when she finds out, but that's just something I'll have to deal with.

Chapter Twenty-Two

Camryn

"So you're trying to tell me someone broke into your apartment and stole all your bills?" Olivia asks, wide-eyed.

I nod. "Yep."

Her expression is one of disbelief, but she closes her mouth and stares straight ahead, blinking.

We're at the gym, walking around the track that's elevated over the entire workout area below. Before she was a married woman, we used to love this vantage point for scoping out the hot guys below. Now, we just walk.

Well, I still look, because *hello*, I'm not dead.

"You probably just misplaced them," Olivia says.

I know that's not true. They were on my dining table right before . . .

Sterling! If he saw those bills and late notices, I'll die of embarrassment. I can only imagine what he must think of me. It's been days since we talked, and honestly, I'm not sure what to think. Last weekend I set him up for that date, and then afterward he came over and we made out like a couple of horny teenagers. I'm sure he's just busy with work, but still, a girl can't help but wonder what's going through his mind.

I told him to go after the woman he was interested in, assuming that he meant me. But now, this radio silence has left me unsure. For all I know, maybe he's still hung up on his ex.

My cell phone buzzes against my thigh. I pull it from the pocket of my spandex workout capris and see it's a text from a certain sexy British troublemaker.

> STERLING: *Are you free on Saturday? I'd love to hang out again.*

A smirk pulls up my lips.

CAMRYN: Is "hang out" a euphemism for . . .

STERLING: Dessert? Yes. Be at my place at seven.

My breath catches in my throat as his bold words stare back at me.

"What is it?" Olivia asks, sensing the change in my mood.

"Nothing," I lie.

With trepidation, I realize this Saturday night could change everything. Three more days until I figure out, finally, what is going through Sterling's mind.

Chapter Twenty-Three

Sterling

Standing in front of my bathroom vanity, I tuck a towel around my waist. After shaving, I rinse my face and apply a splash of cologne to my neck.

My thoughts wander to Camryn, and the level of anticipation I have for tonight is through the roof. All day, my imagination has been running wild with thoughts of what may happen tonight.

Tonight, there's only one thing I know for certain—I want her.

Finally, I run some product through my hair, then get dressed. She'll be here any minute, and though my thoughts are far from innocent, I doubt she'll be amused to show up and find me naked.

I've come to accept the fact that I'm falling for her hard. And I also know there's not a damn thing I can do about it. I'm in uncharted territory, but fuck it, I'm going with my gut. Just like Noah advised, I'm going to be a motherfucking grizzly.

Besides, I have five months to wed, which means I have time to see where things might go with Camryn. If it doesn't work, I still have time to marry.

I can't lose.

My doorman buzzes, and I punch the button on the intercom. A few moments later, I open the front door just in time to watch an unsure-looking Camryn step off the lift.

"Hey there," I murmur, and her gaze darts up to meet mine.

Expectant energy crackles in the space between us. Camryn, looking more beautiful than ever, crosses the hall and steps inside.

"Hi." She's quiet and contemplative tonight, and I can't help but wonder how much of that trepidation is for what may transpire tonight between us.

We grab a couple of bottles of water, and since it's gotten too chilly to enjoy the balcony, we sit together on the couch.

"Does it ever get to you . . . what you do for a living?" she asks.

"Of course it does."

"I'm sorry, that was . . . I shouldn't have—"

"You have this bad habit of apologizing when you don't need to."

"I'm sorry." Her face breaks into a cheeky grin. "Shit. I did it again, didn't I?"

I nod. "Yes, now quit. You can ask me about anything you like. I don't want you feeling like you have to walk on eggshells around me."

She opens her mouth, presumably to say *I'm sorry*, and I shake my head at her, laughing.

Sorry, she mouths with a smirk.

I lunge at her, pinning her under me on the couch, and begin tickling her waist. I dig my fingers into her ribs as I unleash the wrath of my playful fury.

"Not fair . . . so not fair!" Camryn gasps in between fits of laughter. She thrusts her hips up in an attempt to get away, bringing her center in direct contact with my hardening dick, and I grunt.

"Sorry."

This time I don't tease her. "No, you're not," I say, rocking my hips into hers.

A strained breath pushes past her lips, and her eyes slip closed. "God, Sterling . . ." Her voice is almost pained, right on the edge between desire and agony.

"Does that feel good, love?" I push forward again, now fully hard. "When I rub my cock against that pretty clit of yours?"

"Oh, fuck," she curses under her breath. Her eyes drift open, glazed over with wanton lust as they meet mine. "You can't say that kind of stuff."

"I just did, Cami."

With her body restrained beneath me, I'm in the perfect position, and I use it to my full advantage. Kissing her deeply, I rock in tiny thrusts, grinding against her each time we meet.

Whimpers of frustrated need claw up her throat.

"Just feel it, baby." I thrust again, kissing her neck. "Right there."

Her breathing is shallow and fast, her pulse rioting in her neck. The warmth of her penetrates straight through two layers of jeans, and it takes all the restraint I have not to just strip her trousers and knickers down to her ankles and thrust inside her, slowly so I can hear her voice break as she moans.

We continue our game of thrusting and kissing and fumbling until I can't take it any longer. The need to hear her call out my name overtakes everything else.

"I need you," I say on a groan. "Come here."

I sit up, pulling her up from the couch. Her mouth opens but she doesn't say anything, which is good. If she refuses me right now, if she tries to bring rationality to this situation, I might have a fucking meltdown like a two-year-old.

When she stands, I work at the button of her jeans, peeling them and her black satin knickers down her legs. My intention is to strip off her shirt and bra too, but I get sidetracked when I look down and see the most gorgeous cunt I've ever laid eyes on. Shaved bare. Juicy and plump. Wet with moisture that I want to lap up like a dog. *Fuck, I could eat that all night.*

I take her by the hips and lower her to the sofa. "Right here, beautiful." *Sit right here while I eat your pretty cunt.*

If she refuses me, I might just have to spank her. I've never anticipated anything so much as this moment.

Planting one hand under her ass, I use the other to spread her apart with my thumb and finger, exposing the pearl of her clit. Then I lift her to my mouth and lap at her slowly.

"Fucking hell." She moans, fighting to squirm away.

I almost chuckle. Her response is perfection.

But I don't allow her to squirm away. I keep my hands planted where they are so I can taste, lick, suck, and nibble all the sensitive spots that make her moan. Her hips writhe, pushing her against my mouth, and I can't get enough. I've never tasted something so sweet and tempting as her arousal.

When Camryn buries her hands in my hair, holding me in place, I increase my pace. My tongue moves in lazy, yet sure circles over that bundle of nerves that I know will make her detonate.

Soon, she's making sexy whimpers and circling her hips. Gripping both of her ass cheeks, I pull her even closer. Right onto my tongue as I lick her, over and over at a brutal pace.

"Sterling!" She moans my name, tugging on my hair as she comes.

I continue licking and sucking through all the tremors in her sexy body as the orgasm crashes through her. Her body pulses with her release as I kiss my way up to her navel.

And then we're eye to eye.

"Fuck. Did that just happen," she asks. "This is bad. This is really, really bad."

"Afraid so." I'm smug, and I can't help it. I just made her come apart and scream my name in under five minutes.

"Oh thank God, because I was worried I dreamed it."

I can't help but laugh. Damn, she's cute. This must mean she's been dreaming about this moment just as much as I have. It makes me want to do it all over again. As soon as possible.

I help her into her knickers, pulling them slowly up her legs, then help with her jeans.

"Are you ready for that dessert I promised you?"

She clears her throat, looking down at the bulge in my jeans with longing. "What about you? Don't you need . . ."

More than I need my next breath.

"When you're ready."

"Are you sure?"

I nod, wanting her mouth, her hands, more than I want to survive the fucking zombie apocalypse.

"He'll make it," I grit out. *Lie. It's a total lie. My dick is going to die.* "I'll be fine."

"Okay." She smiles at me warmly. "So, you were serious about dessert?"

I chuckle. "Of course." I take her hand and lead her into the kitchen. "You told me once that you wanted to go to Italy."

She shoots me a curious glance.

"I have the next best thing. Gelato."

"Yum."

Camryn squeezes my hand, and we enter the kitchen together. Watching her face light up is worth the extra effort of running across town to the European grocer. My dick is still pissed at me, but my heart is happy.

"I might have even recorded an episode of that show you like. You have time to stick around?"

"Absolutely," Camryn chirps, her cheeks rosy.

Chapter Twenty-Four

Sterling

A few days have passed since my dessert date with Camryn, and my smile hasn't so much as budged.

Sure, I've been working, going to the gym, and dealing with all the other general life stuff, but my mind has been on her. The few times we've spoken on the phone, she says I should go on another date, but doesn't press me when I shrug off the suggestion.

I pass by the lobby, and when I check in with the receptionist, I'm directed to a conference room at the end of the hall. Noah and Olivia are having a baby shower today at their office for work friends. I guess when the two CEOs and marry and produce offspring, it's something their employees want to celebrate.

I figured I'd drop by and say hello. The fact that Camryn will be here has nothing to do with my decision to clear my calendar this afternoon and cross the city for this.

Yeah, right.

When I pull open the door to the large conference room, it takes me a minute to spot any familiar faces. Ninety percent of the attendees are women, and they're all smiling and cooing and talking about baby smells and the best swaddling blankets, and promising that the lack of sleep is all worth it.

Setting the yellow-and-green gift bag on a side table, I cross the room. I had no idea what to get them for their baby, so I opted for something that I hope will make them laugh in the stressful times ahead. Nipple cream for Olivia, and a package of condoms for Noah—size extra-small. Maybe by the time the baby actually comes, it will give me more time to think up a suitable gift.

Spotting the guests of honor seated at the head of the conference table in the very front of the room, I approach and give them each a hug.

"Thank you for coming," Olivia says, her hand on her swollen belly. Her cheeks have a glow to them, and her expression is happy. It's good to see good things happen to good people.

I shake Noah's hand. "Are you kidding? I wouldn't miss it."

Noah shoots me a wry look. "Camryn's over there."

I can't help but chuckle. He sees straight through me. "Thanks. I left a gift on the table. You'll know which one's from me."

"At least have a slice of cake," Olivia says. She's already honing those mothering instincts.

I look over at the huge layer cake frosted in pink and blue that rests in the center of the conference table.

Noah leans closer. "We may have actually conceived on this table. Just an FYI."

Fighting off a shiver, I say *no thank you* to the cake, and go off to find Camryn.

She's standing with a group of women, nodding along to their chatter as she holds a paper plate with an uneaten slice of cake in her hand. I wonder if Noah gave her the same warning.

When she sees me, her eyes widen and she excuses

herself from the group. "What are you doing here?"

"'Ello, love." I kiss her cheek. "I was in the area. Thought I'd swing by."

She smiles at me warmly. "It's nice to see you. Are you behaving these days?"

"Me? No way. Where's the fun in that?" I wink at her.

It's the first time I've seen her since our erotic encounter on my couch. The memory of using my mouth to get her off is one I've replayed countless times. Usually while alone in bed at night. Responding to her breathy moans, moving my tongue faster and faster until she came apart. I want a repeat.

And then we ate ice cream—not ice cream, gelato—while we watched an episode of her favorite TV show. Her contented little sigh as she leaned her head against my chest was perfect. I loved that. Loved holding her in my arms.

Our conversation that night turned deeper. I recall the memories from childhood I shared. How I'd been so mad at my parents for ripping me away from everything I'd known and moving me to a new country. I spent my first years here resentful and bitter, but now it feels like home.

I remember how she almost dozed off at the end of the night. I attributed it to the fact that she must have felt safe in my arms. Then I called a cab for her and sent her home, but she's never far from my thoughts.

Fuck. That's when I know for certain I'm falling in love with Camryn. She isn't like other women. She's driven; she has substance. She makes me want to settle down . . . or maybe I've always wanted that but never found the right fit that would satisfy me mind, body, and soul.

Until her.

And with the deadline approaching fast, I still haven't found a way to tell her how I really feel.

I pause, my hand on Camryn's lower back. "Come somewhere with me."

"Now? What about work?" she asks, her gaze questioning mine.

"Please. I have something I want to show you." Or rather, someone I want her to meet.

She must see something in my eyes, because after a moment of studying me, she grins. "Okay."

Chapter Twenty-Five

Camryn

I'm playing hooky from work, which is totally out of character for me, and I'm practically giddy about it. I feel so rebellious and alive. As I hold Sterling's hand, we practically skip down the New York City sidewalks until we reach a parking garage, where he pauses.

"My car's parked here." He tugs me in after him.

"Are we leaving the city?" I hadn't anticipated driving anywhere, so I'm a little surprised.

"You'll see." Sterling hits a button on his key fob, and a sporty black sedan in front of us flashes its lights.

"A man with a plan. I like it."

We slip inside the cream-colored leather interior that smells so deliciously of his cologne, I almost moan.

"This is me letting you into a new piece of my life." He smiles sadly at me.

"I don't know what to say."

"Say yes. I promise I'll have you home in time for supper."

"Yes."

We drive for forty minutes and cross the bridge into New Jersey. I don't ask where we're going—not because I'm not curious. I don't ask because I trust him, and I want him to know that.

"What band is this?" I ask.

A CD has been playing softly in the background. It's atmospheric rock, and I like the mood it creates— one that's achingly tender and deep, yet filled with possibility.

"It's a band I like called Broken Bells." Sterling looks straight ahead, watching the highway, and I can't help but feel his thoughts are far away.

Finally, we exit and make a handful of turns. I don't recognize the area, and still have no idea what kind of adventure we're in store for. When Sterling slows the car and pulls over on the street in front of a building whose sign reads WESTBROOK ASSISTED LIVING FACILITY, my heart drops.

Everything springs to rushing clarity. It's like opening your eyes after being underwater. This—whatever this is, whoever lives here—this is an important part of his life. And he's choosing to share it with me.

He turns off the car, and the quiet intensity of the moment engulfs us. My hand pauses halfway to the door handle, and when I see that he's just staring straight ahead, I drop it to my lap.

My heart pounds as the significance of this moment sinks in. "Sterling . . ."

Finally, he licks his lips and turns to me. "Maybe this was a bad idea."

I glance at the building again, then back at him. "Are you worried you're going to scare me off, or that I can't handle whatever is in there?"

"Something like that. Just having second thoughts about this."

"I'm not going anywhere," I assure him and take his hand, giving it an encouraging squeeze.

"Okay. Let's do this." His expression is determined.

"Care to tell me what it is we're doing here first?" I attempt a smile.

"Right." He chuckles, opening his car door. "Come on. I'll explain everything."

On the walk into the building, he tells me that his mom has early-onset dementia. He tells me about his dad leaving, and that some days are better than others for his mother. He tells me that when he gets his inheritance money, the first thing he's doing is moving her into a nicer place closer to home. My heart is melting by the time we sign in at the front desk.

Finally, we're directed to room 302.

Everyone here seems to know Sterling; he's a regular fixture here. From the man sweeping the floor, to the nurses, to the director—they all know Sterling. And to them, he's not the handsome and successful attorney who's been in the news lately. He's just a devoted son who loves his mother.

Sterling pauses at the entrance to her door and turns to me, his face somber. "Maybe I should have told her you were coming. Shit, maybe I should have told her *I* was coming." He rubs the back of his neck.

I shift my weight, unable to think of what to say in this moment.

"Never mind. It'll be fine. Come on."

We step inside a dimly lit room. A woman with long silver hair sits in a rocking chair in the corner, reading a book. The room itself is tiny; there's just enough room for a twin-sized bed, a dresser, and the chair she's seated in. A narrow window covered in a dusty drape looks out onto the parking lot below.

"Sterling!" She beams when she sees him. She rises to her feet, and we meet her in the center of the room.

"Mum, this is Camryn Palmer. Camryn, this is my mum, Gillian."

"Pleased to meet you." I reach out and take her small hand in mine.

"I'm charmed, darling." She releases my hand and looks to her son. "What's the occasion?"

He shrugs. "No occasion. I just thought I'd take my two best girls out for ice cream."

Gillian breaks into a happy smile as if this man, her little boy who now towers over her, is her whole world. "Brilliant. Let me get my purse."

We set off, heading to an old-fashioned ice cream shop around the corner. After ordering, we slide into a booth. Sterling sits beside me, and his mom across from us.

It's actually pretty adorable watching Sterling with his mom.

I love that he's sharing a piece of himself that he previously held back. I've tried to deny it all these weeks, but I know now I'm falling hard for him.

Last weekend spun out of control. I never meant to let things go that far, but when the most gorgeous man you've ever laid eyes on wants to pleasure you—you don't say no. And it was amazing. Most guys don't know what they're doing down there, like a vagina is some foreign hostile territory they have to get in and get out of as quickly as possible. Sterling was the opposite. I sensed he actually enjoyed giving me that pleasure, and would have done it for hours if I'd let him. A ripple of heat pulses through me at the thought.

After last weekend, I made a conscious decision not to have sex with him. That's something I can't let happen. I can't give myself to him completely without knowing where he's headed—especially since that might be down the aisle with someone else in a matter of months.

"Tell me, Camryn, what it is that you do?" Gillian asks, pulling me from my thoughts.

Since there's no way I'm telling her that I'm supposed to be playing matchmaker for her son, I keep it simple. "I'm in public relations for a firm downtown. I've been there since college."

"And you enjoy it?" she asks, taking a careful bite of her banana split.

"I love it, actually. I feel very fortunate. And I've gotten the chance to work with Sterling on a special project, so that's been nice."

His mom takes a special interest in me, and my life, and at first I'm not sure what to think. Then I realize it's her way of trying to get to know the woman who her son has just told her holds at least some significance in his life.

"Is that where you two met?" she asks Sterling.

He shakes his head. "I met Camryn years ago through Noah and Olivia."

Gillian smirks. "That Noah is pure trouble." She winks at me. "Too handsome for his own good, and naughty. I had a hell of a time with Sterling and him growing up."

I chuckle. "I bet you did."

"Noah's married now, Mum. With a baby on the way," Sterling says, as though they've talked about that before.

Gillian takes another bite of ice cream, unaware of the look being shared between Sterling and me.

"Oh, there's a movie I'd love to go and see if

you're still coming next weekend, dear," Gillian says to Sterling. "It's called *Indiana Jones*. Looks like something we'd both enjoy."

"Great movie," I say.

"You've seen it? It just came out." Gillian's tone is one of disbelief.

I look to Sterling, confused, and then decide to just go with it. "Yes, I got to see it already. It's excellent. Maybe we can all watch it together sometime."

"I'd love that," Sterling says, squeezing my hand under the table in a silent thank-you.

Soon, we've chatted about movies and our favorite desserts, and even discovered that Gillian shares a love of *House Hunters International* with me. And then suddenly, it's time to go. Sterling's so light and carefree on the ride back to her home, he's whistling.

We drop Gillian off, and she kisses us both on the cheek. "*Indiana Jones*. Next weekend. Bring popcorn."

Sterling chuckles, and we all say our good-byes.

"She's great," I say as we pull away.

"She liked you."

"I think it's admirable how you take care of her."

Watching the road, Sterling stares straight ahead. "I wish I could do better . . ."

"That's what the inheritance is for." That realization is like a pit in my stomach.

He nods.

"Why have her live there if you hate it? Why not move her in with you?"

With a soft sigh that tells me he's given this a lot of thought, he drums his fingers on the steering wheel. "I wish I could. But I often work long hours, and there's too many things to worry about. She could leave the apartment to go to the grocery store and forget how to get home. Forget she left the stove on and cause a fire. There are so many things that could go very wrong."

Glancing at me, he adds, "I don't want to give you the impression it's a bad place. They care for her, provide her with three hot meals a day, oversee her medications, monitor her when she has an episode and doesn't remember where she is. I couldn't do that for her at home. That's why she's there."

"I understand."

"But I want better for her, I want more," he continues. "Somewhere she can garden and go on organized outings, and have her own apartment versus just a narrow room with a bed. A real community, not someplace that feels like a hospital. There's a community an hour away I've set my sights on for her. They have a team of doctors who are on the cutting edge of memory care."

"That's amazing, Sterling."

The elephant in the room that we don't discuss is that in order to make that happen, he and I need to end our charade, and he needs to marry.

Reaching over, I squeeze his knee. "You're doing the best you can. You're a good son."

He nods, now smiling. As the miles tick past, the music plays softly in the background.

It seems a visit with his mom, and seeing the two

of us get along, has done his soul some good.

But there's still something I need to talk to him about. In the excitement of him surprising me at my office and whisking me away on an outing, and then holy crap, introducing me to his mother, I pushed it to the back of my head. Now it's time to get some answers.

"I need to ask you something."

"'Course you can." He strums his fingers against the steering wheel.

"The credit-card statements on my dining table . . . they went missing after you were at my place last weekend."

"You noticed that, did you?"

"You took them?"

I'm shocked and my voice betrays it. I thought, worst-case scenario, he saw them when I went to the restroom, and perhaps shuffled them aside somewhere so I wouldn't be embarrassed I'd left my personal business scattered about.

"Are you upset?" He's still looking out on the

highway, dangerously attractive, but even more so infuriating.

"I'm . . ." *Embarrassed. Horrified.* "Why would you do that?"

He swallows, his Adam's apple bobbing with the effort. "I saw an obstacle standing in your way. Saw an opportunity to clear a path for you. I only meant to help. I'm sorry."

"Wait." I hold up my hand. "What exactly did you do?"

"As an attorney, I occasionally do some work helping people to consolidate debt, file for personal bankruptcy, and things of the like. I got everything arranged with a credit counselor on my team to erase those astronomical interest charges and roll everything into one low monthly payment. You'll be able to pay it off much faster now."

My face contorts into a horrible grimace. Is he fucking insane? He stole my bills, made a plan against my wishes, and now he expects me to pat him on the back?

"I have no idea how it works where you're from, but that was a huge invasion of privacy. It was totally inappropriate, unethical, and just . . . not okay."

He pulls off on an exit and stops at a service station before turning to face me. "I never meant anything by it. Honestly, those are the kinds of things I work on. It was totally normal for me. It didn't feel invasive, or I wouldn't have . . ." He shoves his hands into his hair. "Fuck. Are you angry?"

My heart is still pounding, my pulse racing. I'm pissed off. I feel like he bulldozed his way in and took over, like I'm some damsel in distress.

"Just take me home," I mutter.

After another curse, Sterling hits the gas pedal and speeds off down the road.

The sooner I can be out of the car with his presumptuous ass, the better.

Chapter Twenty-Six

Sterling

What started as a brilliant afternoon turned into utter rubbish. Camryn's angry at me for stepping in to help with her debt, and here I expected to be praised for being so thoughtful. People normally pay me three hundred dollars an hour to do that.

I spent a sleepless night tossing and turning, rolling it over in my mind, and came up with exactly nothing to solve this mess. Watching her interact with my mum? Camryn fits like the puzzle piece that was missing all along. But now I've fucked things up.

Now as I sit in my office, dunking a tea bag into a cup of steaming water, things with Camryn seem as bleak as ever. I've got meetings all day and a client dinner this evening I can't get out of, but tonight I'll find a way to make Camryn understand. Perhaps it's time to tell her how I really feel. *The truth will set you free.*

I press the intercom button on my phone. "Teri, can you come in here?"

My assistant, Teri, steps inside the office, stopping directly before my desk. She's a straight shooter, and I love that about her. And since she plays for the opposing team, there's never been any weird advances or complications between us. It's the perfect relationship.

I remove the tea bag and take a sip of the scalding brew. "Would you mind closing the door?"

Her mouth presses into a line, and she scurries to the door to shut it. "Am I in trouble?"

"Not at all. When have you ever been in trouble?" It's usually me we're plotting how to bail out of hot water.

"Good point." Her smile returns. "So, what's up?"

"I think I might have fucked up."

Teri sighs and sinks into the leather armchair across from my desk. "Is it the Levenstein file, because if I have to fix that one more time, so help me God . . ."

I chuckle. "No, it's not the Levenstein file. It's Camryn."

"That woman you've been spending all your time with?"

I nod, realizing I haven't been as private about the whole affair as I thought.

"What did you do, Romeo?"

"I was only trying to help."

"What did you do?" she says, her voice growing stern.

"I may have taken Camryn's credit-card statements and consolidated them with some help from Brian in the credit department," I say, rubbing the back of my neck.

"Shit. That's a total invasion of privacy, Sterling. You're right. You did fuck up. Bad."

"Thanks," I mutter dryly. "Let's just say she was less than appreciative."

"No kidding. You need to ask someone before you do things like that. Why do you think I can help?"

"Because you know women."

She tips her head, seeming to agree. "Have you tried apologizing?"

I did in the car, didn't I? But Camryn was so angry, maybe she needed time to cool down. I replay our conversation in my head. There's a chance that I just asked her why she was mad and told her I was trying to help. Shit, maybe I never said the two little words I should have. *I'm sorry.*

"You know? That might just work."

Teri's brows dart up, and her mouth opens. "Start with that. Let me know how it goes."

Somehow I know a text message with an apology and a sad-face emoji won't be enough. This is a conversation that needs to happen in person. Face-to-face.

The rest of the day drags by at a snail's pace as I tackle one problem after another. When I finally finish up with the client dinner, I'm crushed to see it's already ten o'clock—too late to show up unannounced at Camryn's place. She's probably in bed.

Not that I wouldn't like to join her, but I know the

best thing is to head home and create a game plan for tomorrow.

Chapter Twenty-Seven

Camryn

"Let me get this straight," Anna says with her hands on her hips.

Leaning back in my office chair, I gesture for her to go ahead. The beginning of a headache stirs in my temples and I press my fingertips there, hoping to stave it off, at least for a few more hours until I'm home.

"So you're mad at Sterling because he ate your pussy and then paid all your bills. Fuck, I'll marry the asshole tomorrow."

Oh my God. When she words it like that . . . Pressing the heels of my hands against my eyes, I take a deep breath and end up bursting out in laughter.

"You can't say things like that, Anna!"

She shrugs. "What? I'm not going to word it all politically correct like you did and say he pleasured me with his mouth. Let's call a spade a spade. He ate that pussy. Now the question is . . . did he do it well?"

"Like that will forgive everything?"

She rolls her eyes. "Yes, because helping with your bills is such a crime."

"He was . . ." *Crap, I can't lie to her.* "The best I've ever had."

She pumps her fist into the air. "I knew it!"

Straightening my posture, I take a deep breath. "That aside, it was a total invasion of privacy, Anna. I was screwed over by the last guy I was with. David had no boundaries, didn't understand that dabbling in my personal affairs was a no-no, and now it seems Sterling doesn't either."

She scoffs. "This is totally different, Camryn. David was up to no good. You need to look at Sterling's motivation and intention. His heart was in the right place."

"Maybe." I cross my arms over my chest. "This whole thing is just getting really complicated between us, and this is just one more thing. I don't know how to feel. And to clarify, he didn't pay my bills, he consolidated them."

She nods, giving me a sad smile. "I get that. So, what are you going to do?"

"He wants to talk to me tonight." He texted first thing this morning, and I agreed.

"Are you okay?" Anna asks, her expression changing to one of concern.

The truth is, I'm not. "I don't know what I'm doing, Anna, and I'm scared."

She nods. "I know what we need to do . . ."

"What?" I ask.

Her gaze drifts to the floor. "You're not going to like this, but I think it's for the best."

Chapter Twenty-Eight

Sterling

After a long day at work, it's already after eight o'clock when I leave the office.

I texted Camryn earlier to be sure she was free for me to stop over tonight. I told her that we needed to talk, and she agreed. Now I'm at the door to her building, waiting to be buzzed in.

Finally, the door clicks, and I pull it open and take the narrow staircase to the sixth floor.

When she answers the door, she's barefoot with a messy bun on top of her head, a woolly cardigan pulled around her shoulders, and a huge glass of red wine in one hand.

"Hi."

"Can I come in?"

"Sure," she says, taking a step back.

I can't help but feel that something between us has

changed. She leads me into the living room, but rather than inviting me to join her or asking if I want a glass of wine, she merely stands there with a hand on her hip.

"I, um . . ." I rub the back of my neck and look down at my shoes. "I came here to apologize." My gaze lifts to meet hers, and what I see staring at me is icy resolve. "I realize that what I did crossed a line. I had no right to step in like that, but I want you to know I was only trying to help."

She releases a sharp sigh. "I know that. I mean, I was pissed at first, but rationally, I get what you were trying to do."

"I truly am sorry." I reach out and touch her shoulder.

"That debt, it's a source of embarrassment. My ex, he . . . you know what? Never mind, it's my responsibility now. It is what it is, and you've probably saved my ass by doing that."

I shrug. "It will save you thousands in the long run, but I should have asked first."

"I forgive you," she says, and those are the

sweetest words I've ever heard.

Camryn swirls the wine in her glass, looking down at the wave of red liquid. "I have something I need to tell you too. I've moved up the event."

"Moved it up?"

She nods. "It's Saturday."

"As in two days from now?"

"Yes." The look in her eyes is sad, like she's made the decision that she can't keep doing this with me.

"I see."

I thought I had more time, but it appears it's all but run out. I wanted to tell her tonight that I wanted to end my search for a wife, wanted to say fuck it—let's call off the whole thing. I'll deal with Charles, figure something out for my mum, but what I absolutely can't do is continue living like this.

But the words lodge in my throat and stay there.

The mood around us changes, grows more urgent, and the gaze she gives me is filled with curiosity and longing.

"We can go over all the details tomorrow after work," she suggests.

"Okay. Let's meet for dinner somewhere."

"Sounds good."

I feel like an utter fraud because we're still searching for my wife, while all I want is Camryn. I'm pretty sure this is the one thing not to do—fall for your matchmaker. But it's entirely too late.

"Tomorrow then." I lift her hand to my mouth and press a kiss to the back of it. Then I see myself out, my heart in my throat.

Chapter Twenty-Nine

Camryn

Blinking into the bathroom mirror at the historic Waldorf Astoria hotel, I heave in a deep cleansing breath.

One more night.

You've got this.

It feels impossible, but I have no choice in the matter. I have to survive one more dinner with Sterling, and then if things go according to plan, tomorrow he'll meet the woman he's supposed to be with and they'll begin dating so that he can meet his marriage deadline. And I'll go back to my lonely existence.

I never would have imagined when I took on this project the depth of feelings I'd develop for the deliciously sexy lawyer Sterling Quinn.

Anna and I went over the plan again today. I'm ready for this. She was right. We had to move it up, force his hand at this, and we each need to move on.

The event is to take place at this very hotel tomorrow morning, in a ballroom on the second floor. I suggested we meet here tonight as a dry run for tomorrow.

I press my lips together, blotting my vibrant berry-colored lipstick, and then head out. As I walk toward the steakhouse located just past the hotel lobby, I smooth my black shift dress over my hips. Fall in New York is my closet's favorite time. This dress is comfortable with its long sleeves and pockets, while still flattering, and I've paired black opaque tights and my tallest black heels. The only color I'm sporting is my lipstick, and the effect is sexy while still being understated.

Once inside the restaurant, I spot Sterling at an out-of-the-way table for two, and start toward him. When he spots me, he rises from the table. His gaze roams up and down my entire body, from my sky-high heels that make my legs look great, to my kissable lips.

Eat your heart out, Mr. Quinn.

We're here to cover the details for the event tomorrow. Not to stare into each other's eyes and fantasize over something that will never be.

That's what my pep talk in the bathroom was all about. No more falling for his swoony charms, sweet smiles, or his positive outlook on life. *No more*. My goal is to get him married—to someone else—then collect my bonus and move on with my life.

"You look . . . stunning," he whispers, pulling me in close for a quick peck on my cheek.

"Thank you."

I take a step back and allow him to pull out my chair. I refuse to comment on how over-the-top sexy he looks. I mean, yes, I'd like to fuck his brains out, but that's beside the point. Tonight I'm playing the role of professional Camryn. In fact, I keep my eyeballs trained on the floor just so I don't stare.

We sit down and glance over the menu.

I plan to order the biggest, juiciest steak on the menu and a loaded baked potato, with plenty of red wine to wash it all down. And, fuck it, I'm even getting dessert. That mountainous slice of chocolate cake I saw on the dessert cart when I came in was practically calling my name. After all, there's no sense in watching my calories now.

Our wine is delivered and we each take a sip. It's delicious, full-bodied and aromatic with hints of cherry and plum.

Then I pull out my file folder containing the details for tomorrow.

Sterling clears his throat, and I expect him to comment on the fact that I'm all business tonight, but he doesn't. He simply pushes the flickering candle aside and leans in to look at the itinerary I've set out.

"The festivities kick off at ten in the morning with an hour break for lunch at noon, and then we'll continue right on through until five p.m., unless you find your Cinderella early. In that case, I have no issues with wrapping up sooner."

He nods once, his gaze downcast onto the paper.

"The hotel will provide security to keep the line manageable, and of course, assist if anyone gets unruly.

The women will proceed from their place in line to one of two tables. They'll meet briefly with either me and Anna, and if we get a sense that she'll be match for you, Anna and I will ask them to wait in a holding room for their meeting with you to begin."

"Sounds good," Sterling says, rubbing the back of his neck.

"I hope there's not too many surprises. Anna and I already spent the last few weeks prescreening the women. And we'll arrive early to make sure everything is set up and running smoothly. You'll have a conference-style room to conduct the one-on-one speed dates in. The setup will be simple—a table and two chairs. I hope that's okay."

"Thank you. This is . . . more than I was expecting."

I nod, accepting his gratitude. "It's fine. I'm just doing my job."

His eyes narrow on mine, like there's something he doesn't like about me calling him a job.

Silence grows around us, and though I've never

been at a loss for words around Sterling before, I am now. He's looking at me like I'm a puzzle he's trying to solve. The server returns with our food, saving me from the awkward moment of silence that seems to stretch out into forever.

Seared steaks with sautéed mushrooms and goat-cheese crostini. Two fresh glasses of red wine. We managed to order the exact same thing again.

"I feel a little foolish. I'm sorry I was babbling on like that, and now we're done discussing everything before the entrées even arrived." I look down at my plate, wishing we'd just wrapped this up with an e-mail, wishing I didn't feel all the conflicted emotions crashing through me.

"Hey." His voice is soft as he reaches for my hand. "Let's not put more pressure on ourselves than is already there. In fact, let's not even think about tomorrow. Please just enjoy this meal with me."

His voice is so tender; it's impossible to say no when he pleads with me like that.

I nod. "You're right. I'm sorry." I take a huge gulp

of air and pick up my fork.

Sterling shakes his head. "What did I tell you about being sorry?"

I smile for the first time tonight. "To knock that shit off."

His chuckle is warm and silky, and I decide it's my favorite sound in the whole world. Hearing this man laugh, there's just something about it.

"Not in so many words, but yes. No apologies tonight. Let's just enjoy a nice dinner and each other's company."

Placing a bite of tender steak into my mouth, I moan. "Dear God . . ."

"Fuck, are you trying to give me an erection in the middle of the restaurant?" he says with a groan.

I swallow, and my jaw drops open. "I didn't . . . what?"

"That little noise you made. And, of course, when you showed up looking like you do in that dress. A man has his limits, love."

"I'm sorry." I wince, realizing I've just broken another of his rules.

He shakes his head as his dark eyes smolder on mine. "You're practically begging for your ass to be spanked tonight."

A sharp inhale is my only response. I can feel my cheeks turning red, so I focus on my meal, cutting up small bites of steak, chewing and swallowing. But the entire time, I'm hyperaware of Sterling's sexy presence across from me.

Somehow we make it through the meal, and then Sterling orders us each another wine and requests the dessert menu.

"My mum's been asking about you."

"Me?"

He nods. "She wants to know when we're all getting together to watch *Indiana Jones*."

I chuckle. "That would be fun. I wonder if we can find a theater that plays old movies."

He rubs his chin. "That's a good idea. I was

thinking I'd have to buy it on DVD or something."

"Soon you'll have enough money to buy your own theater and show whatever kind of movies you want."

As soon as the words are out of my mouth, I wish I could take them back. He gives me a sad look that says part of him wishes this money never came into his life at all.

"I never got to thank you for taking me to meet her. She's a sweetheart," I say.

"I think she liked visiting with you more than she did me." Sterling takes a sip of wine, watching me over the rim of his glass.

The slice of chocolate cake we ordered is delivered with a dollop of fluffy cream and curls of dark-chocolate shavings.

"Oh God, this looks amazing." Tentatively, I pick up my spoon.

"Dig in, love."

I groan. "I've been so good about going to the gym lately. This is not going to end well for me."

"Fuck that. I told you; I like a woman with curves."
He takes a big bite, his mouth moving over the spoon in
a distracting way.

I flash him a challenging smirk. "So you're saying
I'm curvy."

He shakes his head. "Don't turn this into a bad
thing. I'm saying you're perfection. Every man's wet
dream. So eat the fucking cake with me, yeah?"

I laugh, despite myself. "Yeah." Like I can resist,
anyway.

We dig in, and soon we're back to the lighthearted
teasing conversations that I feel like I have only with
Sterling. It feels good, and so normal and easy between
us.

One bite turns into four, and then before I know it,
I've licked the last of the frosting from the back of my
spoon.

"That was amazing." I wipe the corners of my
mouth with my napkin and place it on the table beside
the empty plates.

"Thank you for coming tonight. For dinner, for everything."

"Excuse me for just a second," I say, rising to my feet.

Two glasses of wine and an ice water, and my bladder is yelling at me, despite the fact that I don't want to miss a second of being with Sterling. Somewhere deep inside, I know this is my last night with him.

Once I'm locked inside the bathroom stall, I release a long sigh. I hate that we're coming to the end of the evening. Hate even more that tomorrow, I'll be forced at last to play matchmaker and set him up with another woman. Part of me wishes I could stay at that table, laughing and drinking wine with him, and just be in his presence forever.

In the bathroom mirror, I can't help but notice the reflection looking back at me is somber. Yes, my hair is still blown out into silky waves, and my makeup is still on point, but I can see it in my eyes. There's a deep sadness there threatening to break down.

But I won't cry now. I take a deep breath and drop my tube of lipstick back inside my purse.

When I finish inside the ladies' room, I find Sterling standing in the hallway waiting for me, and I stop suddenly. His presence is dominant, sexy, and the look in his eyes is untamed lust. A dark shiver of need races through me.

He stalks closer and places one hand against my lower back. It's impossible to hold on to the sliver of control I've clung to all evening.

"I'm not ready to say good night, and I don't think you are either."

I blink up at him, intoxicated with desire and momentarily speechless. "What are you saying?"

"Come with me," he says, his voice just a rough growl.

I'm not sure if it's a question or a statement, but without hesitating, I place my hand in his. And then we're heading toward the elevators as quickly as our feet will carry us.

He stabs the button for the fifteenth floor as anticipation races through me. He must have gotten a room for the night when I went to the restroom. Awfully ballsy of him. How he had time to pay our bill *and* reserve a hotel room, I'm not sure.

The elevator doors slip closed, and then we're alone in the small space, my pulse humming. My brain is screaming at me to abort this idiotic mission. There's no way I can be alone with Sterling Quinn in a hotel room and resist doing something naked and slippery.

"You look worried," he says, sliding up beside me. His fingertips are on my chin, lifting my mouth to his for a soft kiss. "Don't be."

His whisper of breath over my lips is so soft and tender, I want to melt into his arms.

After another tender kiss, the elevator stops. When the doors open, Sterling presses one hand against my lower back and guides me down the hall.

We've been building toward this very moment since the first meeting we had at that sexy, swanky restaurant. It suddenly occurs to me—maybe he's wanted this all along.

But why? Am I a distraction from his looming wedding? Or is he as attracted to me as I am to him? And more importantly, is that where this all ends—with physical attraction—and once the itch is scratched, we'll each move on with our lives?

That's the most likely scenario; even my lust-and-wine-soaked brain knows that.

And still, I want this. I close my eyes and make a silent promise to myself. Whatever happens tonight, I vow not to regret it in the morning.

The hotel room is simple, yet elegant. Sterling flips on a lamp, and while I check out the view from the balcony, he excuses himself to the restroom.

I hear the water running, and unsure what else to do with myself, I go to the minibar and grab two glasses. I screw off the top of a miniature bottle of whiskey and dump half of it in each glass, startling slightly as the low rumble of his voice comes from behind me.

"What are you doing?"

"Just a nightcap," I say, raising one glass to him. The truth is, I need something for my nerves. My hands are shaky and my stomach is in knots.

We clink glasses and each take a sip.

Fuck. That burns. I must make a grimace, because Sterling looks at me with sympathy, then takes my glass and sets it on the dresser.

"Come here." His mouth lowers to mine, and his hands slide into my hair.

All the tension, all the worry I had slips away. I forgot what an amazing kisser this man is. He tastes of whiskey and sin, and I want more.

He breaks away too quickly, watching my eyes like he's looking to be sure I want this. I give him a small nod. Taking my hand, Sterling leads me to the bed.

We kiss like that for a long time, our backs against the headboard, his hands on my jaw, our mouths fused together like we're both afraid if we stop, the spell will be broken and we'll have to go back to our real lives. In real life there are sick moms and medical bills, credit-card drama, and obligations a mile long. But here, now, there's only his warm mouth devouring mine in a hungry frenzy. I can taste the smoky flavor of the whiskey lingering on his tongue.

Pressure builds inside as the ache between my legs intensifies. I grip his biceps, loving the solid feel of him beneath my fingers. Corded muscle and broad shoulders, his body is built for sex.

He touches between my legs, lightly at first, and meets my gaze. Within seconds, my eyes slip closed, and my legs part further in silent permission. He moves his hand under my dress and begins rubbing over my tights while I writhe on the bed, wanting so much more. He places my hand on his cock, showing me that he wants me to touch him too. I wrap my fingers around the solid mass, loving the grunt that rips from his chest as I squeeze.

Deepening our connection, he positions us so we're lying side by side. His fingers push past my tights and slip into my underwear. I follow suit, shoving my hand into his pants to find him hard, hot, and ready.

If there's one area he excels in, it's foreplay. There's nothing about this that's rushed. We're still just kissing, our hands roaming as the moment builds.

Sterling is applying just the right amount of pressure, right where I need him, and I break from his kiss to tell him.

"More . . ." I beg.

"I need to taste that sweet cunt again, love." He kisses my lips. "Are you going to come on my tongue again?"

A low moan is the only answer I can give him.

He takes off my dress, and I expect my bra and tights will be next, but he surprises me by pushing my hips backward so I fall onto the bed. The look in his eyes is domineering, almost predatory, as he places his hands on either side of me and leans over my body. Pressing wet kisses on my throat, my chest, my belly, he continues moving lower until I can feel his hot breath ghosting over my center.

Then there's a tug and a ripping sound, and I open my eyes to find he's torn my tights apart, right there, so my pussy is exposed to his hot mouth.

"You're so perfect," he murmurs, pressing a wet kiss three inches north of where I really need him.

I rock forward, unable to stop my body's shameless need to get closer. I remember all too well what that tongue can do.

With his hands on my thighs, holding them apart, he gives me a flirty wink before lowering his mouth.

"Oh God . . ." My fingers thread through his hair, and I'm lost.

His tongue moves in long upstrokes over the entire center of me, and my body shudders. A few more practiced licks and I'm panting with anticipation. I know he's teasing me, toying with me before he begins working me over in earnest.

And then he sets the perfect steady rhythm, a nice medium pace with none of that weird tongue-stabbing thing guys normally do down there, or quick slashes that do nothing but frustrate.

He takes his time. He gets to know what I like. He pays attention to the sounds I make, and adjusts his movements and pace accordingly. Sterling Quinn is a fucking sex god.

He pauses for just a second to give me a pillow, propping me up and telling me to watch, which I totally wasn't expecting. But holy shit, it's hot watching him pleasure me.

With his tongue sliding over my sensitive flesh, his eyes open and lock right on mine. Watching him is so intimate, so raw, I suppress a warm shudder. Then he wraps his lips around my clit and sucks softly, but with enough firm pressure that my hips raise up off the bed.

It's obvious he enjoys what he's doing, and there's something incredibly sexy about that. He gives the impression that he could do this for hours and be perfectly satisfied.

Now that I've experienced Sterling's brand of selfless love, I don't know how anyone else will ever compare.

Blinding pleasure builds, and I soar higher and higher. Sterling's pressure and speed increase until I can't take it anymore. A powerful orgasm rips through my body, hurling me over the edge.

I practically have to pry his head off of my crotch afterward. His tongue continues gentle licks, but it's way too much for me to handle, being overly sensitive from my orgasm.

"Sterling . . ." I grunt, pulling his hair.

He comes up for air, chuckling at me and with a mischievous look in his eyes. "Fuck, you taste good."

While I recover, my chest heaving, Sterling rises and strips off his shirt overhead, and then lowers his pants and boxer briefs, discarding it all in a pile on the floor.

This time it's me giving him a playful shove back on the bed, wanting to show him the same pleasure he brought me. Still reeling and breathless, I lift his heavy cock from where it rests on his belly and give it a slow, wet kiss.

A deep groan of satisfaction rises up his throat. "Wait."

I pause, the head of him at my lips. "What's wrong?"

Chapter Thirty

Her mouth feels incredible, and I don't want to pull away, but I know I need to. With my heart thundering in my chest, I pull a deep breath into my lungs and prop my elbows up on the bed.

"Wait."

Camryn pauses, the tip of my cock poised right at her sweet lips. The sight is so fucking pretty, I want to weep. This beautiful girl, in her ruined tights with her cheeks rosy from the release I just delivered, is ready to pleasure me.

"What's wrong?" she asks.

I'm slightly breathless and a whole lot turned on, but I don't want head because she feels obligated to perform. I respect her too much for that. Everything tonight is on her terms.

"You don't have to do this just because I did."

Her mouth lifts in a smile. "I know that. Now lie back and enjoy, big boy." Her tongue laves over the head of me in one broad stroke, and my eyes sink closed.

"Fuck," I growl, pushing my hands into her hair.

"You like that?" she says, teasing me, her tongue flicking over me seductively.

"Very much." I know for a fact I haven't been good enough to deserve this kind of treatment. She's damn well spoiling me. "Take me deeper, love."

She obeys, opening wide and sliding her lips all the way down my shaft.

"Cami . . ." I groan, thrusting my hips up to meet her on the downstroke.

Propped up, I watch every movement she makes, licking and sucking. Occasionally, she's brave enough to open her eyes to meet mine for a moment before those mesmerizing green eyes sink closed again. She makes little sighs of bliss as if the act of pleasuring me brings her pleasure.

I don't know what I did to convince her to spend the night with me, but I feel like the luckiest bastard alive. All throughout dinner, I kept thinking *this can't be it.* This can't be the end for us, no matter what happens tomorrow. But I won't think about that right now. Because Cami's head is in my lap, my cock buried deep in her throat, and I've never felt so fucking good in my entire life.

She continues moving up and down, and my release starts to build.

"Love." Using three fingers under her chin, I lift her mouth. My cock slides out between her lips with a soft sucking noise, and I groan at the loss of suction. "I need all of you tonight." My voice comes out in a ragged pant as I watch her expression change from one filled with lust to one of deep contemplation.

I would give just about anything to know what she's thinking.

Chapter Thirty-One

Camryn

"I need all of you tonight," Sterling says, gazing at me with an almost pained expression.

The desperate edge to his voice doesn't help. I'm hanging by a thread, ready to give him everything and more. I've left my dignity along with my discarded dress on the floor, and I'm ready to enjoy every moment of our night together. As painful as the thought is, it could be our last.

Sterling rises from the bed and pulls me to my feet. Standing before me, he drops to his knees and peels my ripped tights slowly down over my hips, then my thighs, kissing each inch of skin he exposes. His mouth lingers on my belly, just above my mound. I want his lips lower, but I know he's done teasing me. He's ready for all of me, he said. I can see the look of desire in his dark gaze. This man is desperate to be inside me, and the thought is intoxicating.

And now that I've seen the most perfect cock up close and personal, I want all of him too.

He continues pulling my tights down ever so slowly, over my calves and then over the arch of each foot as I grip his shoulders for balance. With one last kiss to the spot just above my pussy that makes me shiver, he rises to his feet, taking my hand to lead me to the bed.

All of this is new, so I have no idea what to expect, but one thing is certain. He's very much in charge. He sits and leans against the headboard, then pulls me into his lap so I'm straddling him, my knees on the bed on either side of his muscular thighs.

Then both of his arms wrap around my lower back, holding me tight as he kisses my lips and throat, my nipples grazing the firm plains of his chest. He grips so tightly, as if this is a last, fragile attempt to hold on to me. The only way he can truly hold on to me, to what we've started to build, is if he calls off the event tomorrow, but something deep inside me knows he won't do that.

I reach between us, lightly stroking his thick length

up and down, loving the pleased sound he makes low in his throat.

Looking down between us, I frown. "I don't know if you'll fit. It's been a while, and you're, well . . ." *Massive.*

A deeply satisfied smile tugs up his lips. "Oh, it'll fit, love. I'll make sure of that."

His confidence is sexy. Of course it will fit; I just wanted him to know I needed him to go slow at the start.

"Are you ready for this?"

Drugged with lust, I bring the blunt head of him to the juncture between my legs, letting him feel how wet and ready I am. He inhales sharply and grips my ass cheeks in both hands.

We both sigh with pleasure as he finally penetrates me, ever so slowly.

I grip his shoulders, and we kiss deeply as I slide all the way down. The intense stretch of pleasure is almost too much, and I can't help the cry he pulls from my lips.

"Christ, woman," he grunts out once he's fully seated. "You feel fucking amazing."

"So do you," I murmur, my lips on his throat.

"Ready for more?"

I nod, surrendering myself to the moment, to him.

Gripping my ass in his palms, Sterling lifts and lowers me over him, slowly at first, but then with a growing urgency.

Each time we come together fully, I moan at the overwhelming sensation of fullness. In this position, we're eye to eye, making this moment all the more intimate. It's almost too much—our gazes meeting in the dimly lit room, our mouths seeking each other, our hearts beating together.

His pace is so steady and hypnotic, I turn myself over to the desire racing through my veins.

"Ride my dick, baby. Show me how you like it." He laces his fingers behind his head, giving me a challenging smirk.

It's amazing how he can go from sensual, to dirty-talking, to playful, and I love seeing all the sides of him. I don't want this moment to end; it's like magic.

Swallowing a wave of nerves over whether I can perform to his expectations, I place my hands on his shoulders and begin to rock back and forth in his lap.

Sterling's smug smile falls away, and his lips part. "Fuck," he murmurs.

I work my hips faster now, wanting to watch him lose control.

His hands drop to my waist, where he forces me down on him harder, faster.

"I thought you were going to keep your hands to yourself, mister," I tease, my voice strained.

"Not a fucking chance," he growls, lifting one of my breasts to his mouth to taste, nibble, and lick the sensitive peak.

I shamelessly bounce on him, increasing the tempo as our breathing grows ragged and we race toward the finish. Our bodies move together as if notes in a symphony, complementary and never out of sync.

Aren't first times supposed to be awkward and clumsy as you learn what the other likes? This is hands down the best sex I've ever had. It doesn't make any sense.

Releasing my breast from his mouth, Sterling zeroes in on his next target. Sliding one hand between us, he begins rubbing my clit with his fingertips, sending me over the edge for the second time tonight.

My release tears through me, and I grip his shoulders for support as I feel every sensation as though it's amplified through a speaker. It's too much, and yet perfect in its intensity. I shiver in his arms and let him support my weight as he keeps our pace, lifting and lowering me in his lap during the longest orgasm of my life.

As my climax begins to subside, Sterling's pace quickens. A deep groan of satisfaction rips from his throat, and I swear I can feel his cock thicken as he explodes.

Chapter Thirty-Two

Sterling

Camryn is fast asleep in my arms, and even though I have to piss like a fucking racehorse, there's no way in hell I'm moving from this spot.

Tonight was perfection. And I'm not just talking about the sex, though it was hands down the best sex of my life. It was all amazing. From the dinner we shared, where she made me feel so at ease, to her teasing me tonight once we were alone in the hotel room. I love that she's a playful lover. In fact, there are so many things I love about her, as nervous as that big L-word makes me.

And fucking hell . . . the sex.

Watching her pleasure me with her mouth, feeling her come on my cock, the way her muscles tightened around me and she whimpered my name? That was it for me. She's mine, even if she doesn't know it yet.

I was so caught up in the moment, we didn't even

use a condom, something I never do. I know I should talk with her, make sure she's okay, but I don't want to wake her just yet. Needing to hold her a little longer, I tighten my arms around her.

Camryn's head is resting on my chest, and she lets out a sleepy sigh. I hold my breath, unsure if I've somehow woken her, but she merely shifts, nestling in closer.

We crawled under the sheets naked after making love. I look around the room and see that our clothes are still scattered on the floor, evidence of our hurried lovemaking, and two empty glasses still rest on the dresser. Part of me still can't believe she agreed to come up here with me tonight. I figured my idea of reserving a room would be a waste of three hundred dollars, but I was dead wrong.

But what happens next?

The doubt begins to creep in, as do thoughts of my mum. All the plans I made will go to shit if I say *fuck it* and refuse my inheritance.

I've never known a love so pure, so real, and so

right. And that's what I can have with Camryn. I feel it. Deep inside me. When we're together, we're magic. Our personalities, our goals, everything matches. And the mind-blowing sex we just had? That sealed the deal.

But at the same time, what we share scares the ever-loving shit out of me. I spend my days watching couples end their vows. I hear all the stories of infidelity, and even worse are the stories of those who just grew apart. There are no guarantees when it comes to love. Sure, we all try our best, but it's a fucking crap shoot.

Just when I thought I had clarity, things feel more confusing than ever.

I tighten my arms around Camryn, wanting to punch the voice inside me in the fucking face that whispers *this could just be for tonight*.

I may not be sure of my future, but I know if I do marry, I want it to be for love and not money.

There's no road map for where things are headed between us, but when I think about what Camryn brings to my lonesome days—her sweet smiles, her laughter, the unexpected warmth—I know I'm not letting her go.

While we haven't discussed everything yet, she has shared some of the things she wants out of life. I know she wants kids, and I can picture it all, a little girl with her wild, thick waves and spark of fire in her eyes.

I'm terrified I'll mess it up, but when I think about her smart, level head, her passion for hard work, and her loyalty, anything feels possible. I feel confident that with her by my side, I can have it all. I just have to figure out how.

I run my hand along the bare skin of her back and feel her shift as she wakes up, blinking at me.

Chapter Thirty-Three

Camryn

I've just awoken after the most amazing sex of my life. Sterling was so attentive, so giving and loving, and I was so lost in the moment, but now I'm freaking out a bit.

"Cami?" he says groggily, sitting up beside me. "Is everything okay?"

I give him a curt nod but the truth is, I'm not sure.

I rise from the bed, tugging the sheet with me to try to preserve some of my modesty, since I'm butt naked. But of course it's tucked into the ends of the mattress like it's locked in a vise grip. *Seriously*? Why do hotels do that?

I drop the sheet and heave in a deep breath. Sterling's just going to have to see the dimples in my butt and the extra flesh on my belly. But hey, he totally encouraged that cake. He's a cake pusher. Cake pushers can't judge you for a little extra flab. That's like a rule.

"Cami?" he asks again.

"Just a minute."

I pick my dress up off the floor and head into the bathroom, where I close the door behind me. The fluorescent lights are much too bright, and I squint at my reflection. Just-fucked hair and sleepy eyes stare back at me.

When the fuck did he start calling me Cami?

Cami is much too intimate. Cami is a girlfriend. Someone you watch football with on Sundays while scarfing down an entire bacon pizza. But I don't even know if Sterling likes American football. He probably watches soccer. I shake my head, trying to force away the fragmented thoughts in my brain.

I slip my dress over my head, realizing that I have nothing to wear underneath it after Sterling's tights-ripping stunt.

After using the restroom and splashing cold water on my cheeks, I try to compose myself before facing Sterling again.

When I exit the restroom, Sterling's sitting on the end of the bed, and he looks up at me with an encouraging smile.

"You sure you're okay, love?" he asks, his voice soft but steady.

I gulp down a sigh and nod again. The mood in this hotel room has changed drastically in the last five minutes. I was worried about sex changing things between us, and I was right. Things feel different—more complex and cloudy. There are now layers of gray lurking between our once-happy friendship and playful banter.

Shoving my bra in my purse, I slip my bare feet into my heels.

"You're leaving?" he asks, rising to his feet to stand before me. "I thought we'd stay the night . . ."

The gleam in his eyes also says he thought we might fuck again later, but there's no way that's happening. The need to escape is far too great.

"I can't tonight. I need to make sure I'm ready for tomorrow," I manage to say, my voice shaky.

He nods swiftly. "Right. Tomorrow. Of course."

The truth is, I need to be in my own space, need to process this. And I can't wake up next to him and then head off to the recruiting event together. No way. I still can't believe we went all the way tonight. I have no idea where his head is at. Maybe it was just a bucket-list thing on his part—all I was to him was one last hurrah before he has to tie the knot.

"I hope you understand," I add.

"Sure, no worries. Let me make sure you can get into a taxi okay."

A flash of disappointment crosses his features so briefly, I'm sure I imagined it.

I shake my head. "The valet outside will help me." He's still naked, with the weight of his heavy cock hanging between his legs. "I've got this." Heading to the door, I heft my purse strap higher on my shoulder.

His fingertips curl around my wrist just as I'm about to open the door, and he turns me to face him. "Tonight was—"

"I know." I have to stop him; I can't hear him say that it was the best, most amazing night of his life, because I know it was for me. I can't hear him say that and walk away, just to work alongside him tomorrow like this never happened. It's best to turn around and leave, so that's what I do.

Moving as though I'm trapped in a deep fog, I put one foot in front of the other, and then I'm in the elevator under the harsh lights.

All the gray murkiness fades away once I'm standing outside on the curb, tears threatening to spill from my eyes.

I love him.

The way Sterling's scared to believe in love, but still wants to, the way he takes care of his mother, the rough gravelly sound of his voice when we made love, the way he listens to all my opinions and nods, the way he pleasures me like no one else has . . .

I fucking love him.

And I'm terrified about what will happen tomorrow.

Chapter Thirty-Four

Sterling

After rushing home this morning to shower and change, I'm now back at the Waldorf Astoria hotel.

A line of women is wrapped around the side of the building, and I have to instruct my taxi driver to pull around to the back, where I'm let in through a housekeeping entrance so I don't get mobbed. I also have no interest in stopping for questions with the reporters and camera crews who are waiting and interviewing the women.

I head inside, anxious to see Camryn. I barely slept last night after she left. I thought about going home too, but when I lay back down on the bed, the sheets were still scented with her, and some part of me was afraid to leave, afraid that this would all be forgotten once I left.

She never responded to my text when I told her good night, and between that and the hurried way she rushed off, I'm worried about how she's doing.

I've racked my brain and can't come up with anything that I've done to push her away. She's the one who told me actions speak louder than words, and so I've tried to show her what she means to me. Introducing her to my mum, trying to remove the stress of her bills, wanting to spend the night with her, those were all ways I've tried to show her that I value her and want her in my life. If I can just talk to her this morning, maybe I can get her to understand that.

At last, I reach the second floor, and see Camryn and Anna seated at a banquet table at the entrance to a large ballroom.

Camryn is dressed smartly in a black suit and a frilly lace camisole. Her hair is twisted in a no-fuss bun, and she looks beautiful. It makes my chest ache just looking at her.

When I approach, I expect Camryn to rise from the table and give me a hug, but she keeps her head down, leafing through a stack of head shots in a folder.

"Morning," I say to Anna, wondering what's with the sudden change in mood.

"Hi, Sterling," Anna chirps brightly. "Are you ready to find your wife today?"

My mouth goes bone dry, and my stomach does a flip. "Ah, sure."

Anna breaks into an easy grin, as if I've just said something funny. "Today will be great. I promise. Don't look so worried."

I give her a nod. Finally, Camryn looks up at me and seems to study my expression, her eyes narrowing.

"Can I have a word?" I ask.

Without a sound, she rises to her feet and I follow her into the massive ballroom. A huge chandelier hangs from the center of the room, dripping in crystal, and the brightly patterned carpet in creams and blues screams of elegance. I'm sure it's been used for joy-filled celebrations like wedding receptions and inspiring business conferences, but today it feels cold and empty.

"Once they open the doors outside," Camryn says, "this will be the holding room for all the candidates. Then once we've had a chance to screen them, they'll be sent over to the room where you'll be in down the hall for a five- to ten-minute mini-date."

"Sounds like a plan," I say.

When Camryn turns to face me in the center of the room, my first instinct is to pull her into my arms and kiss her, but she's acting so cold and aloof this morning, and she left in such a hurry after sex. I'm not sure my affections will be welcome.

Stuffing my hands in my pockets to keep myself from touching her, I take a deep breath. I realize what I need to do. I just need to get through today. There's a line of women wrapped around the damn building, taking up a city block. Needing a little more time to come up with a plan, I decide I'll play along for now.

"We need to talk after this," I say.

Camryn nods. "Fine. We'll break at eleven forty-five for lunch. We can talk then." And with that, she turns and walks back out of the ballroom.

"Cami?" I call.

She looks at me over her shoulder. "Yeah?"

"Where do you want me?"

"Just down the hall, past the restrooms and the fake plant thingy . . . you'll see it. Good luck." And then she's gone.

My stomach goes from uneasy to *What the fuck just happened?*

I guess it's time to get this shit show started.

Chapter Thirty-Five

Camryn

"Are you all right?" Anna asks when I sit down beside her at the banquet table. "You're acting funny this morning."

"Funny how?" I hope she doesn't suspect anything. I have too much dignity to tell her that I fucked New York's most eligible bachelor last night, a man who happens to be our client.

God, I'm a fucking idiot. I can't believe I thought he was going to call the whole thing off and profess his love for me. I was dead wrong on that one.

"Like you have a stick up your ass or something," Anna says, watching me over the edge of her paper coffee cup.

Her words sting, and I let out a slow exhale. "Let's just get on with this." *Time to put on your big-girl panties and deal.*

"Couldn't agree more. It's Saturday, and we're working. The sooner we hook him up, the better. And then we can go home, right?"

"Yep." Grabbing my phone, I dial the number for the hotel's event manager, who's waiting for my signal before opening the floodgates downstairs. "We're ready. Send 'em in."

Anna rubs her hands together. "Here goes nothing. Let's get that sexy Brit married off."

From our perch at the table, we have a clear view of the escalator, and suddenly here they come, one after the next.

Blond. Brunette. Redhead. Busty. Thin. Young. Old. And everything in between.

Our large printed signs are clear and seem to work. The first women form a line behind our banquet table, a line that soon snakes around the entire perimeter of the massive ballroom behind us.

It's go time.

The first woman in line is standing directly in front

of me, watching me with an impatient smile.

My underarms begin to sweat as the significance of this moment sinks in. Sure, there a few whack jobs here, but for the most part this is an amazing group of girls. By and large, they're educated, beautiful, and looking for love. Or at least they're ready to put their best foot forward for a shot at marrying a millionaire.

It's disheartening to see the idea of marriage boiled down to this. A competition for who has the prettiest smile and can wow Sterling with her wit and charisma.

Anna elbows me in the ribs and clears her throat. "Camryn."

I blink and realize that the line is forming, dozens deep, and I've just been staring off into space.

"Hi. Name, please."

"Brittany Fallon."

My thumb slides along the head shots in the folder until I reach the *F*'s. We required everyone to preregister with us online, so we at least have the basic information and a head shot at our fingertips. I pull her shiny photo from the stack and appraise her again.

Our informal meet and greet with the woman is really just a sanity check. We're making sure that she's a normal girl, someone Sterling might be interested in meeting. The info for the women he likes will be placed into a separate folder, and they'll get a follow-up one-on-one date next week.

I can't even imagine continuing to work on this campaign. *Fuck my bonus. My sanity isn't worth it.* I might have to ask Anna to take over. I don't want to look in that folder and see the glossy head shots and bright smiles of the women, the hope in their eyes at getting the shot to marry a millionaire.

"And what makes you think you'd be a good match with our bachelor?" I ask.

A slow smile spreads across Brittany's lips. "I'm twenty-four with a good job, and ready for a great guy. Plus I love sports, fucking, and beer." She giggles.

"Sold." Anna chuckles. "Head down the hall just past the tree. Sterling will be waiting for you."

What the fuck, Anna?

I roll my shoulders, having no idea what's gotten into me today. Anna, normally bubbly and fun, always makes me smile, but today I want to hit her in the face with a two-by-four.

That was not a proper screening process. For all we know, Brittany could have a pickax in her purse. And the girl is busty and cute, and she just told us she's basically a walking wet dream. She's *not* someone I want anywhere near Sterling.

I watch Brittany strut down the long hall until she reaches the door to Sterling's conference room. A hotel staffer is positioned outside for security purposes, and to make sure only one girl is let in at a time. He's been instructed to give a courtesy knock at the five-minute mark, and to open the door at ten minutes to make sure the mini-dates don't run long.

Nausea rolls inside me as I watch the first woman slip inside the door. I can just picture the sultry smile on her red-painted lips, her come-fuck-me eyes as she bats her lashes at him.

Anna has to clear her throat again for me to realize I'm once again staring off into space as the next girl stands before us.

We manage to get through a couple more in line, sending some to stand in the line that's now formed outside Sterling's door. A few we sent back downstairs, as they weren't a match.

Brittany emerges from down the hall, done with her mini-date, and waves her middle finger straight at me and Anna. "Good luck getting him married off. He's obviously hung up on somebody else."

I barely have time to process her words because we're so slammed with applicants. Bodies are packed wall to wall, and the line grows longer and longer. I'm sweaty and growing agitated, and we're barely ten minutes into our day.

Shrugging off my suit jacket, I motion the next girl in line to approach the table.

Somehow, we make it through the hour or so and a couple of hundred girls. I have no idea how things are going for Sterling, whether he likes any of the women he's met. Other than a text from him an hour ago that said he had something he needed to tell me, we've not had any contact since this began.

Suddenly, Anna rises to her feet and stretches her arms over her head.

I glance up at her, wondering if she needs a bathroom break. We joked with each other about wearing adult diapers today so we wouldn't need to visit the restroom.

"You know what?" she says, fixing her skirt. "Life's too short. You only live once, right?"

"What are you talking about?"

"If you're not going to grab life by the balls, I will."

"Anna?" I ask, my mouth going dry.

"First you let that douche David walk all over you, and now you're just going to sit back and give up on Sterling too?" She shakes her head.

My stomach fills with lead, and I watch in stunned horror as my supposed best friend straightens her shoulders and struts all the way down to Sterling's room, waiting until the security guard opens the door and lets her in.

The fuck?

Did Anna just quit her job for a chance with Sterling?

"Hello? Hellooo?" The blonde standing in front of me wearing stripper high heels waves a hand at me. "Are you okay?"

My heart is slamming against my ribs, and I've broken out in a cold sweat. No, I'm definitely not okay. I just watched twenty years of friendship be thrown away for a shot at a guy. A hot, British, soon-to-be millionaire, but still. If you asked me yesterday if anything could rock my friendship with Anna, I would have sworn on a stack of bibles that nothing could. We were as solid as they come. She knows all my darkest secrets and failures, and she's been there beside me through them all, just like I have for her. And in an instant, that's all over.

"Hello?" Bitch Barbie repeats.

"Just go." I motion her down the hall, feeling like I've now truly failed at everything. At my job, at being a friend, at winning over Sterling. I can feel the edges of a deep depression that's standing at attention, ready to take over the moment I let my guard down.

I send a few more girls away, wondering if Sterling was as thrown off as I was at seeing Anna toss her hat into the ring. I wonder what they could be talking about, and if they'll click.

Finally, Anna emerges from down the hall. She walks straight past my table, her eyes forward the entire time. It's as though she's fighting to hold her head high and make a graceful exit, but I sense that things didn't go quite as well as she had hoped. *Oh, darn.* Then she disappears down the escalator, and I wonder if I'll ever see her again.

I wave the next few girls through without bothering to check their names or pull their information cards. I feel like the world's biggest idiot for setting all this up for the man I've fallen for.

At just before lunchtime, I send a girl in a red dress through to meet Sterling, somewhat aware that she looks vaguely familiar. Maybe she goes to my gym, or then again, maybe I'm just losing it. My entire goal at the moment is to just survive the next few hours and get home, where I'll enjoy a large bottle of wine.

Several minutes later, I check my phone for the time again, annoyed that the girl is going to cut into our one break today. Not that I have any interest in actually eating lunch, my stomach is too twisted up in knots for that, but I just want to go hide away from the crowd for thirty minutes and attempt to get my fucking shit together.

I suspect Sterling's request to *talk* over lunch will be the breakup conversation I've suspected was going to happen all along. I was just a fun distraction, nothing more. And it's not a conversation I'm ready to have. Now or ever.

Realizing she should have been out by now, I rise from the table with a huff and head back to Sterling's room. The security guard is nowhere to be found.

What the hell? Guess he decided to take an early break.

Pulling open the door, I'm struck by several things at once, and my brain struggles to make sense of it all.

First, there's a red dress lying discarded at my feet, along with a tiny black thong. Second, there are soft moans—both male and female—in the otherwise silent room. I keep my eyes cast down on the dress, knowing I'll never be able to un-see Sterling's heart-shattering betrayal.

Just as quickly as I opened it, I pull the door closed and stand there, my mouth hanging open, hot tears staining my cheeks.

The fact that we made love last night makes this moment ten thousand times worse. I feel like my heart has been ripped from my chest and forced through a meat grinder.

With horror, I realize *why* that girl in the red dress looked familiar. That was Rebecca, Sterling's ex. The lawyer from his firm. The one he dated for eight months last year.

It seems he's found his Mrs. Right, someone who can give him exactly what he wants.

The contents of my stomach rising, I run for the bathroom. As I dry heave over the toilet, a cry slips from my lips.

Fuck.

That shit with Anna surprised me earlier, but if I thought that was shocking, it was nothing compared to this moment.

Hot tears sting my eyes as I sink onto the cold tile floor in the stall, sobbing. When that first girl came out of the room, she said he was still hung up on someone. I guess she was right.

Has Sterling been hung up on his ex this entire time?

With disgust, I realize that last night meant nothing to him. I was just a cheap, easy fuck, one last plaything for the manwhore before he's forced into settling down. I fell for his act, the one where he pretended to be a decent human being—funny, humble, and kind—but that's all it was. An act.

Pushing myself up off the floor, I dry my eyes with tissue and make a hasty exit. I make a brief stop at the banquet table, just long enough to grab my purse and cell, and leave all the folders scattered on the table, ignoring the whispers in the crowd as the women still waiting wonder what's going on.

Then I haul ass away from the hotel, needing to be as far away from Sterling Quinn as possible.

Chapter Thirty-Six

Camryn

"What's wrong?" Olivia says the second she opens the door.

I headed straight here to the apartment home of my best friend and boss after leaving the disaster of a PR event I was running.

"What makes you think something's wrong?"

Her gaze drifts to the glass bottle in my hands. "Vodka for lunch is generally a bad sign, no?"

I make a sound of agreement, a sad acceptance of her truth. "Can I come in or what?"

She opens the door wider and motions me forward. "Only if you promise to tell me what's going on."

I nod. I showed up here in a similar fashion six months ago when David and I broke up, and while wine had been my elixir of choice for that breakup, I knew today called for something much stronger.

She leads me into the kitchen to get me a glass of ice and a can of lime soda from the fridge. I open the bottle of cheap vodka because in addition to everything else, now I won't get my bonus, which means my money situation is fucked. The headache I'll have later will be punishment for my stupidity. Pouring a healthy splash into the glass, I fill the rest with soda and take a long sip.

"Come on. Let's go talk," Olivia suggests, leading me out to the living room.

We sit down, me on the sofa and her in the leather recliner across from me. She props her feet up with a smile.

"Sorry. My feet are so swollen, they look like bear claws."

I take another sip of my drink, wondering where I should start. Sterling's betrayal? Anna's? Or the fact that I'm probably going to be fired when Olivia learns what I've done?

"Wait a second." Olivia's eyebrows pull together. "Isn't the event for Sterling today?"

I nod, looking down at my hands. "That's why I'm here. I've fucked up, Liv."

My voice cracks, and I can't hold it in even one second longer. A bitter cry bursts from my throat, and tears began to spill down my cheeks. Setting my drink down on the table, I hug a pillow to my chest.

Then I spill all of it, every ounce of truth that I've kept buried in my heart. I don't stop until I've told her everything—that I went and fell in love with him like a world-class idiot, that we made love, that it was the most perfect earth-shattering sex of my life, that I met his mother, all of it. And Olivia sits quietly listening, her hand on the round bump of her belly.

"It felt so real," I whisper.

She looks at me with a sadness in her eyes. "I was worried about this."

Then I remember her stark warning at the nail salon that day all those weeks ago. She warned me not to fall for him.

"Are you pissed about me ruining the recruiting event?" I was half-afraid to show up here and be turned away, that I'd be told I was going to be fired on Monday.

"No," Olivia says. "Of course not. His behavior was outrageous. And besides, I should have known better than to pair you up. You two have always had amazing chemistry. It was probably a recipe for disaster from the start."

That little admission makes me feel the tiniest bit better, like maybe falling for him somehow wasn't my fault. It was predestined or something.

"Anna's behavior is entirely unacceptable. I'd recommend that we let her go on Monday, if you're on board with that," Olivia adds.

I merely nod. There's nothing about losing a friend and watching her get fired that I find satisfaction in.

Just then, Noah walks into the living room, a red apple raised halfway to his mouth.

I quickly wipe the tears from my cheeks. "Hey, Noah." Taking a sip of my drink, I try to compose myself.

His gaze slides from me to Olivia, and he lowers the apple. "Is this girl talk?"

Olivia nods.

"It's fine; you can come in. This is your house," I say.

Noah still looks wary, like he wants to make an escape but is silently checking with his wife to be sure it's okay.

"Actually," Olivia says as she drums her fingers on the arm of the chair, "we might be able to use your opinion."

I groan inwardly that my very embarrassing truth is about to become public news. This is why having married friends sucks. Nothing is sacred.

"Is it okay?" Olivia asks.

I take a large gulp of my drink, polishing it off. "As long as you keep these coming."

Noah chuckles. "Coming right up. What is it?" he asks on his way into the kitchen.

"Vodka soda, and mix yourself one too, mister," I shout back.

Olivia's eyes widen.

"I'm not drinking alone, and since you're in no condition to partake, that leaves lover boy."

Olivia merely rolls her eyes. "You two are going to be fun to deal with later."

I give her a sheepish smile. "Sorry about that."

"Don't worry. I'll get my payback one way or another."

Noah returns with two fresh cocktails, hands one to me, and then sits down in the chair next to his wife. "Now, what in the fuck is going on that we're drinking hard liquor at twelve . . . thirty-eight," he says, glancing at his wristwatch.

God, it hasn't even been an hour since I discovered Sterling fucking his ex in the conference room. It feels like I've aged sixty years since that time.

While I concentrate on putting a dent in my second cocktail, Olivia fills Noah in on the basics. She spares me the embarrassment of repeating the delicate parts of my story, but Noah's expression goes from neutral to angry, but never seems surprised.

"You knew," I say when Olivia finishes.

"Fuck." He pushes his hands into his hair. "I knew something was going on. But this shit with Rebecca doesn't make sense. He likes you; he really does."

That revelation doesn't mean much. Sterling might have liked me, but not enough apparently.

"Has he ever been known to . . ." Olivia pauses, looking at me with concern.

"Go ahead," I say, encouraging her.

"Has Sterling ever been known to hook up with someone like that, randomly, practically in public?"

The look on Noah's face says it all.

"Spill it, Noah. The truth," Olivia demands.

"In the past, yeah. There was this time several months ago when we volunteered at a soup kitchen. He banged a girl in the bathroom."

Olivia's face twists in disgust. "He fucked a homeless person? Does the man have any standards?"

Noah shakes his head. "No, she was another volunteer there for the day."

"Guys, this isn't helping."

"Right. Sorry." Noah rises to his feet. He returns with a bottle of vodka and a fistful of takeout menus. "We need to turn this into a proper post-breakup pity party. Pizza or Chinese?"

I laugh despite the crappy mood I'm in.

"Both," Olivia says, grinning.

Later as we sit there, eating plates of egg rolls, lo mein, and pepperoni pizza, Noah offers a solution.

"I could just call Sterling. Find out the truth of what the fuck happened today."

In my buzzed state, I consider it for a second. It's not a half-bad idea.

"No way," Olivia says. "He'll try to talk his way out of it, then he'll want us to put Camryn on the phone.

So, no," she repeats. "He needs some time to sit and ponder what he did wrong. There's no redemption for him tonight. Let him suffer in silence."

She already made me turn off my phone earlier, and then hide it somewhere in her kitchen where I won't be tempted to see if I have any missed calls or voice mails.

Noah and I have put a hefty dent in the bottle of vodka, and I know later I'll eventually be faced with the decision to cab it home or stay the night in their guest room. But there's something about being inside their happy home that makes me feel out of place.

Maybe it's just that they're married, and their love is a real, visceral thing I can feel in the space around us, or maybe it's just because I'm so far from anything similar in my life. It hurts when I pause to think about it. Which is why I need to just keep drinking.

I don't know what tomorrow holds. I only know that I won't be working with Sterling on his search for a wife ever again.

Chapter Thirty-Seven

Camryn

I managed to keep my phone turned off all weekend, and now I'm back at work on Monday morning without knowing whether Anna or Sterling tried to contact me.

I almost caved a thousand times. Not that I would have contacted him. But I stood at the kitchen counter, my finger poised over the power button to my cell for a long time on Sunday. The pull to know if he'd tried to contact me was so strong. Would there be a text from him to say he was sorry? Would there be an explanation that, after facing all the women, he decided he wanted to get back with Rebecca after all?

It was better not knowing. For now, at least.

Navigating my way through mass department e-mails and other things of nonimportance, I stifle a yawn as I try to unclutter my in-box. The comforting morning ritual, paired with a steaming cup of coffee, makes me feel halfway human again. A long weekend spent sulking wasn't healthy. My work gives me purpose, so at least there's that.

I'm still wondering if Anna's going to be brave enough to show her face here today. And I have no idea what I'll do if she does, since I'm assuming clawing her eyes out and calling her a cunt is against the employee code of conduct.

At a few minutes before eight, Anna enters the office. Rather than the confidence she radiated on Saturday, holding her head high as she strutted past my table, today she wears a subdued expression.

"Hey," she says sheepishly. She enters the office but stays near the door.

My gaze lifts to hers, but my fingers remain on the keyboard. My hope is that this is quick and painless, that maybe she's just here to pick up her belongings.

"Can we talk?" she asks.

I tip my chin. "Sure. Say what you need to say." *It's not going to change a damn thing.*

I have too much respect for myself to be like *Hey, you betrayed me? That's cool.* I may forgive her in time, but the trust is gone. And friendships without trust are like bachelorette parties without alcohol—they're not something I want any part of.

"I got caught up in the excitement of the event. I mean, really, that's a compliment to your skills as a publicist."

When she gives me an awkward smile, I think I throw up in my mouth a little, but I keep my expression neutral, still willing to hear her out.

Since I don't say anything, she presses on.

"The idea of marrying a multimillionaire, and not to mention that he's hot and British, I just couldn't let all that pass without at least trying. I hope you understand that."

Now I'm just starting to get mad. Not once has she said she's sorry. These are all flimsy excuses.

I take a deep breath, making sure my voice is calm and in control. "I have work to get done, Anna. Is there a point to all of this?"

She shifts her weight from one high-heeled foot to the other. "I just wanted to make sure you're not mad."

At this, I almost laugh. And not because it's funny, no. I'm talking a full-on maniacal Disney-villain laugh, because she's clearly insane.

"Mad?" I rise from my desk. "Let's see. You deserted me at a work event to try and pick up a guy. A guy, despite all the mitigating factors, you knew I had feelings for. So, no. Mad doesn't even begin to cover it."

Her mouth opens and she takes a step back.

"I'm not simply mad. I'm furious at your behavior, disappointed at your lack of apology, and quite honestly, floored that you had the gall to show up here today asking if I was mad. We're done, Anna. And not only that, but we're done working together too."

"You're firing me!" she cries, her voice rising in disbelief.

"No, I'm not firing you. That was Olivia's call. It turns out, when you want to keep a job, you should, I don't know, do what you were hired for and not flake out on the people who are counting on you." I've crossed the room so I'm now standing directly in front of her with my hands on my hips. "Good-bye, Anna."

With an annoyed huff, she spins on her heel and storms away, making a disgruntled noise as she goes.

I heave in a breath, my knees trembling despite how composed I might have seemed.

Just then Sterling rounds the corner, his hands moving lazily together and apart in a slow clap. "That was bloody brilliant."

My mouth twitches in a smile. It actually felt damn good standing up for myself. I don't relish the idea of losing a friend, but as the saying goes, with friends like that, who needs enemies?

Anna and I have been close since elementary school, though these last few years we've grown apart. Somehow, I know life will go on and we'll each lick our wounds and eventually get over it. Hell, maybe we'll even laugh over this someday over cocktails, but I doubt it.

But I don't have time to reflect on what just went down with Anna. Because Sterling is standing before me in a tailored black suit looking mouthwateringly, soul-crushingly, chest-achingly beautiful.

Stay strong, Camryn.

"Did you need something?"

"Aye. I came by to speak with you about Saturday." He's breathless like he ran the whole way here. And maybe he did. His office is across town.

My gaze drifts down to the red and green folders he's holding at his side.

Unlike Anna, he's not here to make amends. He's simply trying to follow up on our project—the shared goal we had of getting him married off. It seems he's made his selections. The green folder is for those women he'd like another date with, and the red one holds the turndowns. It seems he followed directions well.

As hard as the words are to say, I force them out. "Come on in."

I head back to my desk, sliding into the rolling leather chair while Sterling takes the seat across from me. He sets both folders on my desk. The red one is about five inches thick, bursting with head shots. The green folder looks like it could be empty for all I know.

"I tried to reach you all weekend," he says, his voice soft.

I press my lips together, trying not to say something that involves the words *fuck* and *you*. *Be professional, Camryn. Just get through this.*

"I'll get this handled." I reach for the green folder but Sterling flattens his palm against it, holding it in place.

"I just don't understand what happened," he says.

Inhaling deeply through my nose, I try to calm down. But after dealing with Anna, my tolerance for bullshit is practically nonexistent.

"What happened was I'm an idiot. I have a job to do, and I let my emotions get in the way of that. It won't happen again." My tone is cold, and if I could pat myself on the back for sounding so aloof, I would.

Sterling's eyes are dark, stormy, and conflicted. "I

was falling for you."

"And see, that's where I call bullshit. I saw you and that girl Rebecca. Your ex."

His dark brows draw together, and his perfectly kissable lips part as his expression changes to one of confusion. "What exactly did you see?"

What did I see, exactly? "There was a dress on the floor. And I heard moans."

He nods, not denying it.

"Why didn't you just admit to me from the start that you weren't over your ex?"

"I had no idea you saw that. The only thing I knew is that your friend Anna threw herself at me, and then you were gone."

I look down at my hands. "I saw, Sterling. And then I left, because I just couldn't do it anymore."

"Let me explain a few things to you," he says, his tone precise. "For some strange reason, my ex, Rebecca, was allowed through the screening process, which made little sense to me because I had previously communicated to you that I had no interest in her. As in, none."

He leans forward, his hands gripping the edge of my desk. I look up, and his dark eyes are filled with regret.

"She came in, stripped out of her dress, and turned on a porn video on her cell phone. It was a desperate and shameless attempt to get under my skin. I opened the door, wanting her to be removed, but when I found the security guard gone, I went in search of someone to help. I knew Rebecca wasn't leaving without a fight. And the last thing I wanted was to be in the same room with my naked ex, and have you walk in on that and assume the worst. Which is apparently what happened."

My windpipe threatens to close. Dear God . . . I thought they were in there fucking like rabbits. My eyes wouldn't let me look.

"And that was after I'd been proposed to eight times, and asked for my credit score, my blood type, if I was into double penetration or bestiality, was willing to have my palms read, and one crazy broad wanted to check my cock for warts."

"Holy shit. Are you serious?"

"Deadly. It was quite a fucking morning."

"So you didn't fuck Rebecca?"

"God, no."

I take a deep breath. "Was there anyone nice and normal who you liked?"

"There were a few who seemed like nice girls, but no, I didn't like any of them. It turns out, I've already given my heart to someone else."

I swallow, so badly wanting to believe he's talking about me, but I won't let myself go there just yet.

"And to top it all off, you were gone. Nowhere to be found."

"I'm sorry about that. I thought you were in there fucking Rebecca. And after what we shared Friday night . . ." My mouth goes dry, and I can't continue.

"I understand. I get it. It was just a really tough weekend to get through. I thought you weren't speaking to me because of the whole Anna thing. And I want you to know, I had no interest in her whatsoever. Even less after I realized how little she values loyalty and friendship."

"It was a difficult weekend for me too."

Losing Anna was unexpected. But spending all weekend mourning the loss of the fragile foundation I'd built with Sterling was worse. I recall what Noah told me about Sterling having been known in the past to engage in random hookups with women he'd just met. And even though nothing happened this time, I'm still on edge about what that could mean, what kind of man he is underneath the shiny exterior I've gotten to know.

"I want you to know that Friday night meant everything to me."

I can't look up and meet his eyes. I don't trust myself.

Instead, I stammer, "No matter what happened between us, I vow to see this through till the end. I'll be a professional and won't let anything get in the way of you getting what you want—a wife."

"You really are an amazing woman, Cami." He

smiles at me fondly with that guarded tenderness I've grown to love.

I motion for him to hand me the green folder. "I'll get dates set up for this week with your finalists."

"Sure," he says, handing me the folder before turning to leave.

I draw in a long, slow inhale as my frayed nerves threaten to riot and send me into a tailspin. I'm thirty minutes into my Monday, and so far I've fired Anna and then had Sterling tell me that he didn't lay so much as his little finger on Rebecca, let alone stuff his cock inside her. And I believe him. I just do.

I stare at that folder for a long time. Then I set it aside and attempt to finish the e-mail I was writing.

Fuck it.

Knowing I won't be able to concentrate until I see what's inside, I grab the folder from my desk.

Slowly, I open it and find the picture's turned over, so only the back side of the glossy photo paper faces me. With trembling fingers, I lift one corner and flip it over.

For several seconds, I just stare at it blankly, my brain struggling to comprehend.

It's me.

The photo is one of me. Taken when I sat across from him and his mother in the booth at that ice cream shop, a dot of whipped cream on my lower lip and a smile in my eyes. He'd snapped it with his cell phone, and I never thought anything of it.

But now it feels like everything.

Except . . . what does it mean?

Chapter Thirty-Eight

Sterling

I wanted to give Camryn some time, so I've kept myself busy with the mountain of work on my desk, but now it's after five and my heart is in my throat.

I grab my leather carry-all, cell phone, and suit jacket, and head out. The New York City streets are filled with weary commuters and cyclists and cabbies, all jockeying to get through the throngs. They long to be home with loved ones. There are wives to kiss, children who need a bath, crying babies who miss their mothers, and meals to be enjoyed at tables all around the city. It's something I've never taken the time to consider, but on this cool fall evening, I feel more alone than I have in a very long time.

I could call up a mate, go to a pub, enjoy a pint, and maybe even pick up a girl to bring home. But the only girl I want is Camryn. I could go visit my mother. Except what if she's having one of her off days, and doesn't recognize me? I don't think I'm game for any more rejection right now.

I've spent years telling myself I don't want to settle down, that matrimony is for fools. But seeing these people around me, rushing to get home to loved ones while I have nothing, it's a stark dose of reality. I hop on the train that will carry me to my building and check my cell yet again. Still nothing.

I finally decide to text her.

STERLING: Can we talk tonight?

I stare at my phone for several seconds, hoping her response is positive and immediate.

But my phone remains sadly silent. Briefly, I consider going to the gym instead of going home. I keep a spare set of clothes in my locker there. Lifting weights and jogging around the track would be better than sitting alone at my apartment, but I decide I don't have the energy for that.

I'm emotionally exhausted, and I'm beginning to

think, maybe this is it. Maybe this really is the end for Camryn and me. A man can only hold out hope for so long before he gives up. But I've never been a quitter, and part of me refuses to accept this is the end.

Just then, my phone buzzes in my hand.

> *CAMRYN: I'm on my way home from work. But yes, I think we should talk.*

Her message gives nothing away, and of course I'm dying to know how she's feeling, what she thought when she saw her photo in that folder.

> *STERLING: I'll meet you at home. That okay?*

> *CAMRYN: Sure.*

My heart starts pumping in earnest. I could fist-bump the guy sitting next to me, but I refrain. I haven't been this fucking excited since she agreed to share my hotel room Friday night.

By the time I trek all the way across town toward Camryn's flat, it's almost seven. I stop and grab a bottle of white wine and a pint of ice cream. We've both probably missed dinner, and in times of stress, there's no better dinner than sugar and alcohol. At least, that's my theory.

When I finally make it to her door, Camryn answers, still in her work clothes—a royal-blue silk blouse that reminds me of the color of the British flag, and fitted black pants that hug her curves. She looks beautiful. The only change from when I saw her this morning is that she's ditched the nude-colored high heels and is barefoot.

Without those killer heels she favors, she looks so small and vulnerable. I hate to think that she was hurting all weekend after thinking I'd hooked up with Rebecca. Quite the opposite—I called security on her ass, and she left kicking and screaming obscenities at me.

"Can I come in?"

She opens the door wider. "Yes, sorry."

We've both sort of spaced out, our eyes drinking in the other after a long, weary day.

I follow Camryn inside and set the shopping bag on her counter. "Have you eaten dinner?"

She shakes her head, still watching me curiously.

"I brought wine and dessert."

"For dinner?"

I nod. "It's not gelato, but it should do the trick."

"Sounds perfect." She gathers two wineglasses and two spoons while I use her bottle opener to uncork the wine.

We take everything out to the couch as if by unspoken agreement. Sitting next to her TV is a stack of DVDs of the reality show *The Millionaire Matchmaker.*

"Really?" I chuckle, motioning toward the DVDs.

She shrugs, digging her spoon into the now softened chocolate ice cream. "It was research."

There are so many things I want to say to her, but I have no idea how to begin, so for a few minutes we sit in silence, taking turns spooning heaping bites of ice cream directly from the pint.

Setting my spoon aside, I pick up my glass of wine and take a sip. "How was your day?"

She takes one more bite of ice cream, then sets her spoon next to mine on the coffee table. "After letting Anna go, and then trying to pick up where she left off with some of our clients, it was stressful. Thank you for bringing this by."

"Did you happen to look in the folder?" I ask, growing impatient.

She takes another sip of her wine and then sets it down on the table. "I did."

Her tone is subdued, and I have no fucking clue what to make of that.

"And?"

She turns to face me on the sofa, her fiery green eyes looking sad. "And I have no idea what it means.

You want to marry me? You want to date me?"

I reach over and take her hands, folding them in mine on my lap. "I want a relationship. I want you in my life. After everything—getting to know you, introducing you to my mum, trying to deny my attraction—I'm done. None of those women held a candle to you. You're the only one I want."

She pulls her lower lip between her teeth, looking unsure. "What about the inheritance?"

Inhaling sharply, I squeeze her hands. "I don't know, but I won't live a lie or deny myself any longer. I want to make you mine."

Pulling her into my arms, I lean forward and kiss her, softly at first, then deeper as her body molds to mine.

She pulls away suddenly, placing a hand on my cheek. "I have no idea if I'll be ready to get married five months from now, and in fact, I doubt I will be. And besides that, the idea of marrying someone so quickly is a little insane, no offense." Her hand falls away, and I miss her sweet touch almost instantly.

"None taken. It's scary. I get that more than anyone. Marriage is a huge leap of faith, and I never thought it was something I would take on."

"But now . . . because of the money?" Her tone is uncertain.

"Fuck the money. I won't be controlled by it."

"But what about your mother?"

My gaze drifts away from hers. "I don't know."

She nestles in closer to me, and I know we can both feel it. Love is scary and unpredictable, and neither of us wants to lose what we've just started to build. I tighten my arms around her possessively, unsure what might happen next.

"I need you, Cami. Tell me if you don't want this, say it. Tell me no."

She doesn't say anything, instead she rises from the couch and takes my hand, tugging me up after her. Pulling me silently behind her, she leads us to the bedroom.

Standing inches apart in the center of her bedroom,

I meet her gaze with hungry desire. The last rays of the evening sun are gone, and the glowing lamp on the end table creates a dim glow around us.

Taking my time, I strip us of each piece of clothing in turn.

I remove her shirt, my fingers grazing the lace of her bra, then pull my own shirt overhead, placing her palm against my chest.

Next her pants and silk knickers are stripped off, and I grip her cute arse in my palms, giving it a firm squeeze. *Mine*, I want to growl. Instead, I shove my trousers and boxers down, then bring her hand to my steely cock. Her fingers curl lightly around me, and I grunt out a breath.

"Cami . . ."

She strokes me lazily up and down like we have all the time in the world.

"That feels really fucking good." I groan, bending down to kiss her neck.

Palming her full breasts, I enjoy the way her breath

catches in her throat when my thumbs graze her perky nipples.

Wanting more, I take her hand and guide us to the bed, laying her down before me. I plan to thoroughly worship her tonight.

I taste her lips, feel them part and hear her groan when my tongue meets hers. Then I work my way lower, kissing her slender throat, the valley of cleavage I create with my hands, then her soft belly.

She's perfection. Every inch of her, inside and out.

Reaching between her legs, I'm pleased to find her wet, and tell her so. A little whimper is the only response I get, not that I was expecting one. As I massage her clit with my thumb, her whimpers increase in volume, transforming into moans as I press harder.

I could toy with her all night. But I won't, because believe it or not, my cock has needs too. Still, a gentleman always ensures his partner gets off first, and that's one rule I will never compromise on when it comes to Cami.

Slowly, I slide two fingers deep inside her snug

body, pushing them in as far as they'll go. She's warm and tight, and so lovely. Watching her eyes drift closed as I fuck her with my fingers, I grab a fistful of her hair, tilting her head, and take her mouth with mine. My cock twitches with the need to be inside her as I slide my fingers in and out in a maddening rhythm.

"Wait," she says on a moan. "Sterling . . . wait."

Pausing with my fingers still buried inside her, I break from the kiss to meet her hazy eyes.

"Make love to me," she whispers.

"Do we need to grab a condom?" I ask, one hand on her cheek, the other still fucking her.

I recognize that last time, in the heat of the moment, we didn't use a condom. Today, I'm more prepared with a couple of the buggers stashed in my wallet, but remembering the way her bare skin felt against mine, I'm hoping we can forgo them. Guilt should have been the only emotion I had after fucking her without a condom the first time; instead, my only thought was *again*. The idea of putting something between us is maddening.

She cocks her head to the side, considering it. "It's okay. I trust you. And I'm on the pill."

Sliding my fingers out slowly, I bring them to my mouth, sucking them clean. "So fucking sweet, Cami." I'm dying to taste her again, to feel her body quake as she comes against my mouth. But I need her just as badly as she needs me.

Positioning myself over her, I hold my weight on my elbows while Camryn reaches between us and brings me to the warm, wet slit between her legs.

Heaven.

"Slow," she begs as I begin to press forward.

"Are you sure?" I tease her, sinking in just an inch, then pulling back again.

She lets out a frustrated grunt, angling her hips up. "More."

Thought so, love. I want to laugh, but she feels so fucking amazing as I sheath myself in tight, hot velvet, I let out a ragged groan instead.

Reaching down to grip her ass in one hand, I

roughly pull her onto my cock each time I thrust. Soon, I'm buried deep and we're both breathing hard.

What began as something sweet and tender has turned intense and passionate. I pound into her again and again, and Camryn cries out, scratching my shoulders and back as she fights to hang on.

I grip her tightly as though I'm holding on to a precious treasure. "That's it, baby. You like that?"

"Yes," she cries. "More, Sterling, more."

Giving her every ounce of pleasure I can, I rock into her, our desire building.

"I love you." I groan, kissing her neck.

"I love you too." She sobs out the words, her lips seeking mine.

She clings to me as her climax rushes through her, and feeling the way her body tightens and milks me, I follow her over the edge.

"Baby, you okay?" I brush her hair back from her face and kiss her swollen lips.

"I'm much better than okay. Holy shit, Sterling."

Chuckling against her lips, I pull out slowly, groaning as I withdraw from her body.

As I clean her up and watch her lounge in the bed, I think to myself what a lucky bastard I am.

Crawling back in beside her, I tug Camryn close. I have no idea what's going to happen next, but I know I need her in my life.

Chapter Thirty-Nine

Camryn

Sterling and I are spooned together under my sheets. It's just after daybreak, and we've both got to head off to work in a little while, but I wish we could stay like this forever.

We didn't get much sleep last night. If I thought last Friday was good, that was merely a taste of what this man can deliver. It turns out he can go for hours. And then some.

We had sex, cuddled, had sex again, ordered pizza at midnight, ate naked, then took a bath. Then we made love slowly, and slept for all of four hours. It was heaven. The best part wasn't all the sex, although that was perfect. It was hearing Sterling tell me he loves me. I still don't know what happens next, but I hope we can face, together, whatever happens next.

"You awake?" he asks, his voice groggy.

"I think so," I whisper.

He turns me around in his arms so we're facing each other. "Morning, love."

I smile up at him. "Morning."

He presses a kiss to the tip of my nose and smiles back at me. For a moment, I fear I've done things totally backward. I've fallen in love with Sterling, slept with him—numerous times now—all before we were even officially dating. That was in stark contrast to the proper order, according to my matchmaker research.

But then I tell my inner voice to stuff it. I'm happy. That's all that counts, right?

Rolling over, I heft myself up from the bed.

"Hey, where do you think you're going?" Sterling's arms wrap around my waist as he tugs me down on top of him.

"To shower. We've got to go to work, right?"

There's a mischievous glint in his eyes. "I'm suddenly feeling quite ill. Think I might have to call in sick and stay in bed all day."

My mouth lifts in a smile. "Oh, really?"

"What do you say? Olivia will understand, won't she?"

I've very rarely taken a sick day. I actually don't think she'll mind, given everything that's happened. Plus, when your boss is also your best friend, there are a few perks.

"What will we do all day?" I ask with a smirk.

"I can think of a few things . . ." Sterling's palms slide up my thighs and I squirm, ticklish under his skillful touch.

"You're going to be trouble, aren't you?" I place my hands on his firm chest, loving the hard ridges of muscle I find, and push back against him. Of course, my efforts don't even budge him an inch.

"We can stay in bed until late morning, go out to breakfast, maybe take a walk in the park, come back, nap, fuck again." He grins. "Like a real couple."

"Sounds dreamy." I chuckle.

"But first, there's something I want to tell you." His voice turns serious, and I lift my head from the spot

I've claimed on his shoulder to meet his gaze.

"I need you to know that I want to marry for love, not money. And I know this might scare the shit out of you, because it's surprised the shit out of me, but when I think of being married, the only woman I see standing beside me as I make those vows is you." He meets my eyes as his fingers trace lazy circles over my hip bone. "I never expected to want this. But I do."

My heart jumps into my throat, and I'm not sure what to say. Is he proposing? We're naked, for fuck's sake. And I wasn't even certain if we were dating.

"But," he continues. "I want to wait."

All the breath pushes out of my lungs, and I don't know if I'm relieved or worried. "Wait?"

"And not because I actually want to wait," he says. "I would make you mine tomorrow if I could. But because I want to show you that marrying you has nothing to do with getting my inheritance. A smart woman once told me that actions speak louder than words, and so that's what I intend to do, to date you for however long it takes to show you that I want you as my wife." His fingertips dance over my skin so lightly, they burn. "I want to wake up next to you every day and make love to you every night. I want to take you to Italy and put little babies in your belly. I want to grow old with you, Cami."

Tears are freely streaming down my cheeks. I was wrong before about the nickname Cami. Cami isn't a girlfriend you watch football with on Sundays. Cami is a *wife*, someone you build a life with. Cami is the name you call out from the baby's bedroom because his diaper has exploded and you need backup. It's the loving nickname you whisper in the dark when you need to know you're not alone. And I can see all of that and more in his loving gaze.

"Say something," he whispers.

I take a moment, trying to find my voice. "Life is hard. Adulting is hard. Sometimes it sucks, actually." I wipe my cheeks with the back of my hands, drawing strength as I speak. "But facing it together? Having you at my side? The man who makes me laugh, who makes every gloomy day seem brighter just by being in it?"

I pause to collect myself. My throat is so tight, and

more tears threaten to escape. But these are happy tears. Sterling swipes under my eyes with his thumbs, and I take a deep, steadying breath.

"The man who makes love like a porn star, who makes me insane with desire . . ."

He leans in and steals a quick kiss.

"Of course I want this. At whatever pace feels right for us both."

"That makes me so fucking happy," he says with a groan.

"Wait." I sit up suddenly, tugging the sheet up to cover my breasts. "You're not marrying me for a green card, are you?"

At this, he bursts out laughing. "No, love. I live in this country legally. But that was cute." He tugs the sheet from my grasp. "Don't hide those beautiful tits from me again. I'm practically your husband."

A bubble of laughter rises in my throat at the absurdity of it all, but then Sterling's hot mouth closes over one nipple, and my laughter fades into a low moan.

Chapter Forty

Camryn

Nearly five months later

"Are you sure about this?" Olivia asks, navigating the stairs to the hotel in sky-high heels. She looks amazing for having a three-month-old baby strapped to her chest. I swear, nothing slows her down.

"Positive." I grin.

Looking down at my engagement ring, I feel almost giddy at the thought of deceiving everyone. I didn't want a big rock or a lot of fanfare, though Sterling wanted to spoil me. When he proposed in Central Park, he did so without a ring. It was Christmas in New York, which means it was that magical time of year where everything is filled with joy and cheer. Big white fluffy snowflakes falling from the sky, us huddled together in wool coats and scarves, drinking hot cocoa and watching the figure skaters on the ice rink. It's a memory I will always treasure.

He dropped down to one knee with a sweet, short, and genuine request that I make his life complete by becoming his forever. He asked me with a shaky voice if I would be his wife.

While tears filled my eyes, he pulled off my mitten and kissed my left ring finger. When I sobbed yes, he told me he wanted us to pick my perfect ring together. We went into Tiffany's beautiful New York store, my cheeks pink and my eyes watery with happy tears. They gave us champagne and let me try on every ring I wanted. I could tear up again right now remembering Sterling's happy smile.

The sales staff teased him about proposing without a ring, saying that it was a brilliant plan just in case I said no. But when our gazes met, Sterling and I both knew there wasn't a chance I would have said no.

I ended up selecting a simple, yet sturdy platinum band encrusted with five rows of diamonds. It was two carats, but all the diamonds were tiny flecks encircling the ring. The effect was so sparkly, and the significance of there being no beginning and no end held meaning for me. Sterling picked a similar style ring, thick platinum without any diamonds. To my surprise, he's worn it every day since. I teased him and told him in this country that engaged men don't wear rings, and he simply said *I know.*

"Well then, let's get on with it. You have a groom to deceive," Olivia says, pulling me from my daydream. Her hand pats Emma's back softly as she coos to her daughter, who's almost asleep.

Suddenly, my thoughts darken. "Oh God. I just thought of something. What if Sterling thinks I planned all this, that I'm only marrying him to get the inheritance money?"

Olivia chuckles at me. "You just now thought of that?"

"Yeah. Why?"

She shrugs. "That's what I've been worried about the entire time."

"Fuck." I push my hands into my hair. "Am I slow or something?" I've never even considered that.

"You're not slow." She laughs. "You're in love. It

clouds the brain; not your fault at all. I think it's cute."

At the word *cute*, I roll my eyes. Just great. My fiancé, who wanted to wait to marry, is currently out with Noah for drinks, and I'm at the hotel panicking.

We're in Vegas for what he assumed was a bachelor party for him, but really, we're getting hitched tomorrow at noon at one of those cheesy drive-through chapels. Then we'll have dinner with our best friends, Noah and Olivia, and there will be dancing and champagne, and then a whole lot of sex in our hotel suite later. I'm practically fucking giddy just thinking of it. Five months of dating hasn't even begun to cool the insatiable lust I have for him.

We've had our ups and downs like any couple, there have been mundane things like dealing with stress at work, and busy schedules, and then there's been the tougher stuff, like watching him suffer as his mom's health worsens. I thought our names might be dragged through the mud when the media learned that New York's most popular bachelor was dating his matchmaker, but there was only excitement as the will-they, won't-they aspect of us marrying took center stage.

But there have been countless sweet times too. Sterling is a loving boyfriend, thoughtful and considerate. He's an amazing lover, and my best friend. I hate to think where I'd be today without him. Probably a bitter, jaded, and very single version of myself.

I love him, and that means I care for him enough that I won't allow him to miss out on inheriting fifty million dollars simply to prove a point. I know what that money could mean for his mother's care, and for our future. I'm not marrying him for the money; I just hope he knows that.

My stomach tightens when I remember how set he was on the notion that we wouldn't marry until later. He wanted to be absolutely certain I understood that he wasn't marrying me so that he could get his inheritance. But now, standing here, doubt has started to creep its way in. Maybe he's just not ready . . .

I guess there's one way to know for sure.

Chapter Forty-One

Sterling

"Deeper," Camryn whines.

"I'm trying, love," I say with a grunt.

There's an anxious edge to her voice, and I press in further.

"I can't find it." Sweat is beading on my forehead and my arm is buried up to my elbow. I push in deeper, the need to please my woman outweighing my discomfort. *Fuck.* Still nothing. "I'm in as far as it'll let me, love."

"My hands are smaller. I'll have to do it," she says.

Pulling my arm free of the sofa, I stand up.

"Are you sure you lost your phone there?"

She shakes her head. "I was sitting on the couch, and that's the last time I remember seeing it."

Checking the hotel suite, I return a moment later

with her phone in my hand. "It was on the bathroom counter."

"Oh."

"Are you okay? You seem really jumpy today."

Her gaze drifts to the floor and she nods. "Fine."

I smooth my hands over her shoulders, rubbing the tension I feel there.

I wonder if she realizes, like I do, that tomorrow marks the six-month deadline. Maybe that's put her on edge, though I'm not sure why it would. We agreed to wait to marry, and I feel more confident than ever that it was the right thing to do.

We can take our time and plan something special where all of our family and friends can be included. When you know something is going to last a lifetime, there's no sense in rushing it.

Before, I was in a hurry to get to the altar, to sign the papers and be done with it. But love has changed everything. It's given me a fresh perspective, and now I see that all the money in the world won't make my life any better than it is. As long as I have Camryn by my side, we'll figure the rest out.

"Come here, love."

She lays her head on my chest as I fold her into my arms.

"Tell me what's bothering you," I say.

She shakes her head. "It's nothing, Sterling." She wipes her eyes quickly with the back of her hand.

I'm not sure of the right words to say to ease her mind—hell, I'm not even sure what's on her mind—so instead, I do the only thing I can think of.

I take her to bed and make love to her until all she can feel is me.

• • •

"Babe?" I say, my voice shaky. "What's this?"

Our limousine has stopped in front of one of those tacky drive-through wedding chapels. The neon sign outside promises weddings in fifteen minutes or less.

The smile on Camryn's face falls when she meets

my confused expression.

"Surprise," she says weakly.

Noah and Olivia sit stoically across from us, seeming afraid to move or breathe.

"I don't understand," I say. Now Camryn won't even meet my eyes.

The limo driver opens the door and offers Camryn his hand. "Miss, we're here."

She tells him that we'll need a minute, and he closes the door.

"Cami? What's going on?"

She swallows and takes a deep breath. "This all seems rather foolish now, but I—"

"Noah, Olivia, would you mind giving us a bit of privacy?" I say.

They nod and exit the car, leaving Camryn and me alone. The faint scent of leather and the hum of the air-conditioner are our only companions.

"I love you, Sterling. I wasn't going to let you

throw away the chance at your inheritance. I know you thought that was the right thing to do, but I'm ready. And I think you are too."

"So you brought me here . . . to get married?"

She nods.

Holy shit. I never saw that coming. Maybe I should have, given that we're in Vegas, but when she said it was a quick getaway with friends for a bachelor/bachelorette weekend, I believed her.

Pushing my hands into my hair, it takes me a moment to know how to respond.

"Sterling . . . Say something," Camryn pleads.

"I need a minute here, love."

Camryn reaches out and squeezes my knee. I see the outfit she chose now with new eyes. The cream-colored lace top and black skirt is what she chose to get married in. Her lips are painted matte red, and her shiny black pumps elongate her legs, making her a little closer to my height.

I just can't believe she planned this whole thing

without telling me. We tell each other everything.

"Do Noah and Olivia know why we're here?"

She nods.

My gut is churning, and I'm trying to push away the negative thoughts playing in my brain. She'd never marry me for the money. This is Cami.

"Sterling, you know I'd never push you to do something you weren't ready for."

She told me that she needed commitment, that she was looking for her lobster. And when I realize that I've been denying her simply because I was trying to prove a point, I feel pretty fucking selfish.

I lift her hand to my mouth and press a kiss to her palm.

"Baby, when I put that ring on your finger, I meant it. I want you today, tomorrow, and forever. If you're sure about this, then let's go get married."

Camryn's mouth breaks into a happy grin.

• • •

It was every bit as cliché and sappy as you can imagine, and we laughed and kissed and smiled through the whole thing. And now fifteen minutes later we're back in the limo, the ink drying on our marriage certificate.

Camryn's in my lap, her ass is in my hands, and her lipstick is staining my throat and the collar of my white shirt. But it's fine. She's mine and I'm hers, and I don't mind her marking me.

"We did it. We freaking did it." Camryn grins.

"Love you so much, baby." I say, pulling her lips to mine again.

"Love you more," she coos.

Noah and Olivia share an uncomfortable look. "Geez, at least wait until we're back at the hotel to hump," Olivia says.

"Then you better tell the driver to step on it," I say. Because I can't wait to make love to my wife.

Epilogue

Camryn

"Cheers," Sterling says, raising his glass to mine.

"To?" I clink my champagne flute against his, watching the wind tousle his hair that's grown too long on top.

"To being newlyweds, and millionaires," he suggests.

"That's a good one." I lean forward and press a kiss to his lips.

It's crazy how much my life has changed. I'm now Mrs. Camryn Quinn, and my sexy new husband and I are enjoying a month-long honeymoon on a private yacht in the Mediterranean.

I may have thrown him for a loop, planning a wedding and not telling him, but after coming home from Vegas, we set about planning our honeymoon and attended to some personal affairs. Sterling got his mom situated in an amazing community with the best doctors anywhere. She has her own apartment with a little garden in the back, where she spends most of her time. We visit her every weekend, and sometimes meet up with her for dinner during the week too.

With my bonus, I was able to pay off the credit-card debt that had haunted me. It was important to me that I use my own money, from my job, rather than because I was lucky enough to marry a millionaire. Though admitting to Sterling that the debt was due to my ex was almost more embarrassing than him assuming I've made poor decisions. As I suspected, he never judged me, though he did want to hunt down David and kick his ass.

Sterling reaches over and gently tugs on the string to my bikini bottoms.

I can see the look of raw hunger in his eyes, and I smile at him. Most of our days have been like this. Filled with sun and sea and flirting and lots of lovemaking.

"Let's go below deck and see how many times I can make you come, riding my face."

I chuckle. "Maybe later, lover boy. It looks like we're headed to that marina."

Sterling's gaze swings portside. "Brilliant. We're here."

"Where?" I ask. The green hillside is still a mile away, and the few buildings I barely make out in the port are minuscule.

"Italy."

Happy tears fill my eyes as I realize this amazing man has made all of my dreams come true.

If someone told me six months ago that I'd be married, I would have laughed. If they told me it was to the cocky player, Sterling Quinn, I would have punched them in the nose.

Of all the unlikely scenarios I could have imagined, this was never one of them. And yet everything has unfolded naturally between us. Despite all the chaos and drama the impending inheritance brought us, everything clicked between us right from the very start.

I guess sometimes things are just meant to be.

Now Available

ROOM

The last time I saw my best friend's younger brother, he was a geek wearing braces. But when Cannon shows up to crash in my spare room, I get a swift reality check.

Now twenty-four, he's broad shouldered and masculine, and so sinfully sexy, I want to climb him like the jungle gyms we used to enjoy. At six-foot-something with lean muscles hiding under his T-shirt, a deep sexy voice, and full lips that pull into a smirk when he studies me, he's pure temptation.

Fresh out of a messy breakup, he doesn't want any entanglements. But I can resist, right?

I'm holding strong until the third night of our new arrangement when we get drunk and he confesses his biggest secret of all: he's cursed when it comes to sex. Apparently he's a god in bed, and women instantly fall in love with him.

I'm calling bullshit. In fact, I'm going to prove him wrong, and if I rack up a few much-needed orgasms in the process, all the better.

Acknowledgments

There are so many wonderful people who support me in this writing journey. Most of all, I want to thank you, the reader. Thank you for picking up this book and giving it a chance. I know there are so many choices these days, and you have my gratitude. I love being an author, and I couldn't do it without the wonderful readers like you.

My husband is a constant source of encouragement, and for his love and unwavering support, I am so grateful. Thank you for being my rock, baby.

I owe a tremendous amount of thanks to the following ladies:

Rachel Brookes. Oh my God, you sent me a lobster mug after reading the first draft of this! I'm so blessed by your friendship, and the wisdom you share each time I send you a rough manuscript. Thank you for loving Sterling.

Emma Hart and Sofie Hartley, two amazing Brits who read this and helped me shape Sterling's character so that he was authentic and deliciously British! Thank you also to Franci Neill for your early read through and notes.

Natasha Gentile, thank you for always being there to read through and provide your careful insight, quick humor, and a funny GIF or two. Your encouragement means the world.

Danielle Sanchez, my right hand and trusted advisor, I'm so thankful for all that you do. We're never ever breaking up, okay?

Pam Berehulke, I am so grateful for your wisdom and grace. Your editing skills can't be matched, and I'm so lucky to have you in my corner.

About the Author

A *New York Times*, *Wall Street Journal*, and *USA TODAY* bestselling author of more than twenty titles, Kendall Ryan has sold more than a million e-books, and her books have been translated into several languages in countries around the world. She's a traditionally published author with Simon & Schuster and Harper Collins UK, as well as an independently published author.

Since she first began self-publishing in 2012, she's appeared at #1 on Barnes & Noble and iBooks charts around the world. Her books have also appeared on the *New York Times* and *USA TODAY* bestseller list more than two dozen times. Ryan has been featured in such publications as *USA TODAY*, *Newsweek*, and *In Touch Weekly*.

Other Books by Kendall Ryan

Unravel Me

Make Me Yours

Working It

Craving Him

All or Nothing

When I Break

When I Surrender

When We Fall

Filthy Beautiful Lies

Filthy Beautiful Love

Filthy Beautiful Lust

Filthy Beautiful Forever

The Gentleman Mentor

Sinfully Mine

Bait & Switch

Slow & Steady

Hitched Volume 1-3

Hard to Love

Reckless Love

Resisting Her

The Impact of You

Screwed

Monster Prick